Peri Christian had the house to herself that afternoon, which was just the way she liked it. She only wished it could have been a permanent arrangement. Her father and stepmother were at work and Nicola wasn't back from Guiseppe's Pizzeria, where she had gone to guzzle pineapple, pepperoni and mushrooms with her friends, Amy and Ellie.

Peri hated pizza. Pepperoni stung her mouth and the cheese was gluey and stringy — she didn't know how Nicola *could* eat it. But then, she didn't know how Nicola could do a lot of things. They didn't have much in common. Damn it, they didn't have anything in common, except their father. Nicola was Peri's half-sister. Nicola had other half-siblings called Jo and Duncan who weren't related to Peri at all.

Looking back through her mental telescope Peri could pinpoint the exact time when she had realised that her big brother wasn't her brother and how much that realisation had hurt. She had really liked Duncan then but these days she found it safer not to like anyone too much in case they let her down. The only person Peri *really* liked and trusted was Skates.

Strictly speaking, Skates was a dog, not a person, but ever since Peri had acquired him as a straight swap for a pair of in-line skates she'd considered him proof positive that sometimes you *could* buy love and loyalty. If you looked at him objectively, Skates was rather an ugly dog but Peri thought him perfect. She snapped her fingers and Skates, who'd been half-asleep, immediately bounced up and came over to rest his chin on his knee.

'What do ya reckon, Skates?' asked Peri, and Skates wagged his silly stump of a tail.

Yes, Skates was definitely better value than her family — if you could call it a 'family'. Mr and Mrs Christian, Duncan and Jo Graham, Peri and Nicola Christian, and hardly two of them related to any other two! If Peri's dad had done the right thing, cut his losses and stopped at one wife, Nicola would never have existed. Of course, Peri couldn't remember her mother at all — she had been only a baby when Mrs Christian, the first, had taken off.

Peri wasn't sure how she felt about her mother. Sometimes she thought, good for you, Ma! because the idea of being tied down with a squalling kid and dirty nappies did nothing for her either. Other times, she thought it was a bit rough, being dumped like a stray kitten on her dad. And her dad couldn't have liked looking after babies either, because he'd gone right ahead and married Carolyn Graham, mother of Duncan and Jo. Then they'd had Nicola just to totally cock up the 'family'. Talk about his, hers and theirs!

Peri's lip curled and she held the expression in a freeze frame. Wasn't that always the way!

'Shove over, Skates.' Peri reached down to pick up a magazine and flipped through the pages until she came to the fiction segment. Yes, there it was — a heroine sneering at an overbearing hero. And a few pages later she'd be melting in his manly arms. Peri closed her eyes and melted into the cushions, arms flung back in elegantly curled abandon, hair carefully strewn over the arm of the couch. She adjusted the angle of her head and winced as an earring caught in the fringe of a cushion. Maybe that second set of holes hadn't been a good idea.

'Less is more,' quoted Peri, and snorted. 'Not for this kid, Skates!'

Sweet simplicity might be Nicola's style — it wasn't Peri's. If old Carolyn didn't keep her so short of money, she'd show her a thing or two about style. She'd finally get to make up the garments she designed in her spare time. Make them properly, in good quality materials instead of the el cheapo remnants old Carolyn made her use.

Old Carolyn. That was what Peri always called her stepmother in her mind. Once upon a time, in the good old days, she had called her *'Mum'*. But Nicola and Jo and Saint Duncan called Mrs Christian *'Mum'*, so Peri wasn't going to do it, too. She had nothing in common with her stepmother and as soon as she could scrape together some cash, she'd be moving out of home.

Peri stretched further out on the couch and grabbed a cushion off the floor, held it to her chest and wrestled it.

'Darling, *darling*!' she squealed, and let out a few moans for good measure. 'Aaghh! That's so *good*!' She rolled back and forth and finally slithered right off the couch and onto the floor where she continued to writhe and kiss the cushion until she was breathless. That was a good trick, she thought, examining the lipstick stains she had made on the cushion cover. That had sounded very realistic — that's if you could believe all you heard on TV. Peri didn't believe half of it. She'd kissed a few guys in her time, down on the beach, away by the waterfall, and it had done nothing for her at all. It had all been pretty disgusting, really. They had damp hands and wet, sloppy tongues, and they were always groping about her ribs, trying to find a way in through her shirt. Let one of them get a hand on her breasts and they'd squeeze them like oranges. Peri Christian wasn't an orange, and she didn't want some guy's tongue in her ear. The next one that tried that was going to get it right where it hurt. She moaned again, and looked at the clock. If she could only know exactly when old Carolyn would be coming home, she could lock the door and go through the whole performance again, fortissimo. That would get her going.

Peri yawned. God, another term and a bit of school! And then, with luck, she'd be out of Surfside High for good. Of course Dad and old Carolyn wanted her to stay on and do Year Eleven. Of course they did! Duncan and Jo had, and now Duncan was a qualified music teacher and Jo was a chef. Great. They'd never catch her dead being a music teacher or a chef. Clefs and beats to the bar, cleavers and asparagus, silly hats and stupid students. Peri had other plans for her life. Leave school, get a job, leave home and start *living*. Have enough cash for make-up and fashion and style. She'd been a cruddy schoolgirl long enough.

The only trouble was, she still hadn't the remotest idea of what she was going to do. She'd get good results in English, Design and Maths, but what could you do with those? She'd fail Japanese and Australian Studies, and probably Art as well. Only a cretin could fail Art, they said, but Peri's ideas didn't match old Oilrag's at all. The only thing she really liked was fashion design, and you couldn't just walk into a job like that. She supposed she could start out by selling pizza at Guiseppe's — if the manager, John, would take her on — but she hadn't exactly been his greatest customer. He was more likely to give Nicola a holiday job ... and here *came* Nicola singing up the path, off-key, as usual. Why couldn't the girl shut up and face the fact she was totally, totally tone-deaf?

Peri shook her head angrily and culled a few more expressions from the magazine. Smouldering desire, like the girl on page 17. A sexy pout, like the heroine of the second story. Peri pursed her lips and half-closed her eyes. 'Kiss me...' she breathed.

Then the door burst open and Nicola came in, and her peace was at an end.

CHAPTER 2

The last week of third term was limping on. Peri found herself prowling the corridors of Surfside High like a caged panther. That was how she thought of herself, anyway.

She could feel the sparks of annoyance glancing off her ears, and sizzling off the ends of her hair. It was like going about with her head in the middle of an invisible, inaudible sparkler. She couldn't get away from it, but nobody else seemed to notice it at all. The rest of the population just went about their business, mooning over the hunks in Year Twelve, discouraging the weeds in Year Eight, running late for assembly, running early for recess and driving Peri mad. It was a time when some teachers beamed at the students with determined good cheer, others were hassled and bad-tempered with the pressures of all the work they had to get done by the end of the year. Nearly three terms gone and only half the curriculum covered! Panic! Peri hated both sorts of teachers. She didn't feel like being polite to the beamers and she wanted to snap back at the dragons. But when she did, she landed in detention.

'It's bloody wrong,' she said angrily to Nicola that night. 'They can snarl at us all they like, but if we put a foot wrong they clap us in detention. There ought to be a law against it. There *is* a law against it, if you're an adult. Just catch an employer being allowed to lock you in an office — you could get them for sexual harassment!' Peri was only talking, but Nicola took her seriously, as usual.

'Why don't you join the student council, like Cadi Merrick and Aaron Wilkes?' she said. 'That way you get a say in things like that.'

'You've got rocks in your head,' said Peri savagely. 'You know the sorts of things *they* discuss?'

'Rules and things,' said Nicola vaguely.

'Let me give you an example. One of their latest debates with Mr Goodhew was whether to recommend that the canteen offer more interesting menus or stick with the lentil soup. And did they come up with any wild ideas for decent food? *No!* They bloody well recommended that we should be allowed to buy pizzas on Wednesdays! *Microwave* pizzas! Big deal! You can get better pizzas at Guiseppe's — if you like that sort of muck at all.'

'But if they'd come up with wild ideas, Mr Goodhew would have said no straight out,' said Nicola. 'This way, they might get some concessions.'

'Concessions! God!' said Peri through her teeth. 'That canteen needs a bomb under it! Healthy food's all very well — but does it have to be so horribly boring?'

'Changes have to come slowly.'

'Yeah? Tell that to the Industrial Revolution. Or to Russia!'

'And look at the mess *they're* in,' said Nicola smartly.

'Oh — piss off!' Peri snapped.

'Girls, girls!' said Carolyn Christian mildly. 'There's a time and a place for everything, and my kitchen is not the place for swearing. Have you done your homework?'

'Didn't have any,' muttered Peri.

'Gee, you kids have got it easy, said Peter Christian. 'When *I* was in high school we slaved over our books all day and every night.'

Peri wanted to tell him to piss off, too but one bout of detention was enough for one day. She sneered at him instead. 'Did the poor widdle boy have to work in the salt mines then? And was he forced up chimneys by his howwid old master?'

'You bet,' said Mr Christian good-humouredly. 'And beaten, we were, regularly every Monday.'

'Come on, Pete,' said Mrs Christian with a smile. 'It wasn't that bad.'

'Wasn't it — I tell you, you couldn't pay me to go back to school!'

His wife flicked him a warning glance and Peri smiled sourly. That's it, Carolyn, she thought, don't let him tell us what he really thinks about education. Make him tell us what *you* want us to think he thinks. And sure enough, her father laughed sheepishly. 'Oh well — I suppose it wasn't all bad,' he said. 'I quite liked some subjects.'

'And if you hadn't gone on to Year Eleven you wouldn't be where you are now,' said Mrs Christian meaningfully.

'God, you're so transparent!' said Peri with disgust. 'Dad's doing contract paint jobs — he didn't need Year Eleven for that — hell, he probably didn't need Year *Seven* for that! It's a matter of work experience. This is all about me leaving school, isn't it,' she continued. 'Well, isn't it? Come on, Carolyn — you can't tell me you went on and did Year Eleven and Twelve. You've gone on often enough about how you were a hairdresser at sixteen and married at nineteen.'

Her stepmother's face went cold, but she managed a smile. 'And look where that got me,' she said pleasantly. 'Divorced a few years later with no qualifications since I didn't finish my apprenticeship! Not a path I'd recommend you girls to follow.'

'What about my real mother?' argued Peri. 'She didn't even last two years with Dad. And didn't she go to university? Proof positive education screws you up.'

'This is a totally fruitless discussion,' said Mr Christian. 'Now, if you two don't have any homework, you can do the washing-up.'

'I have some Japanese to finish,' said Nicola, 'and a project on Chechyna.'

'Peri can do it then,' he said.

That was just typical, Peri thought. If only she'd admitted to the essay she had to write, she could have been let off the washing-up, too. Now, she had to either suddenly 'remember' the essay or do two jobs. No — three, because she still had to walk Skates.

In the end Peri decided to skimp on the essay. Everyone knew the teachers didn't bother to mark most of it — they'd all formed their opinions of the various students' abilities and attitudes already, anyway. As long as she attempted to do the work, that was enough. As for her attitude, they could like it or lump it. There were only about ten more weeks left to go before she was shot of school for good — if she could get her father to agree. Old Carolyn didn't matter — she was only a stepmother, but her dad, though he was easygoing most of the time, had a habit of putting his foot down, hard, on occasion and then — look out!

'I could leave school and be your apprentice, Dad,' she said hopefully while stacking the dishes.

Mr Christian choked on his coffee. 'Not on your life!'

So even her dad didn't want her. Great.

Nicola came and helped her with the washing-up after all.

'I'd make a good contract painter,' Peri said, as much to convince herself as Nicola.

Nicola laughed. 'You'd end up with paint on your boobs if you leaned over too far.'

'Just because you're first cousin to an ironing board ...' Peri retorted.

The wrangle over that lasted them nicely until the last knives and forks were put away.

CHAPTER 3

There was an assembly on Tuesday afternoon. Peri thought about sloping off to the toilet and missing the whole boring thing, but she knew the loos would be full of kids with the same idea — and half of them would be having crafty fags. They'd be out on their ears if they got caught, but most of them were no-hopers who didn't care.

Peri swaggered into the auditorium and propped herself against the back wall. She'd make sure she was the last one to sit down, then she could disappear if it got too boring. Unfortunately, she wasn't the only one with the same idea. Bonner Shaw was there, too. On the look-out for people who were looking for trouble, not so he could join in, oh no! Just so he could blight their fun. And he was coming over to talk to her. Peri snarled at him and he back-pedalled quickly. Even Bonner could take a hint if you beat him over the head with it.

Having seen off Bonner, Peri leaned back against the wall. She slid her fingers under the ledge of the speaker mounted on the wall just by her left shoulder and unparked a wad of chewing gum. She had left it there last assembly, and there it still was. Proof that cleaners didn't clean. Peri inspected the wad swiftly for any unsavoury additions, then popped it into her mouth for the ceremonial chew. This one lump of chewie had lasted her all term — she had a bet with herself she could leave it parked at the end of the year, come back in February and find it still there. But she wasn't coming back, not if she could help it, so she might as well chuck the chewie in the bin.

Peri sighed loudly, and gave the evil eye to the back of Nicola's head. Her stupid half-sister had taken to wearing her long fluffy black hair skinned back in a tight braid. Somebody ought to tell her it made her look like a wuss.

Peri wondered what had made Nicola do it, then she saw Cadence Merrick pushing her way along the row. Light dawned. Cadence was two years ahead of Nicola, in Year Ten. She was one of the kids who always succeeded at everything. Drop Cadence in a sewer and she'd come up smelling of Chanel Number 5. Cadence was Ms Perfect, Ms Brains and Ms Nice. Peri Christian hated her guts. And now the girl had her claws in Nicola.

Cadence had a habit of making friends with kids from the lower years, especially the meek little mice. She'd take them up and they'd think she was wonderful, for a while. They'd all start busily turning themselves into carbon copy Cadences, complete with skinned-back hair — although, Cadence had Barbie doll curls around her face, daisy earrings, designer bike shorts and all. The only thing was, Cadence had the looks and figure to wear that stuff — most of the kids she adopted didn't, so they ended up looking like pathetic skinned rabbits.

Cadence disciples never lasted long. She was just too much to live up to — too good at everything, too kind to people who weren't up to her standard. Peri wondered when Nicola would see the light, but considering she'd hate it if Nicola tried to talk *her* out of anything, she'd keep out of it. Anyway, Nicola could stew in Cadi-juice for all Peri cared. It would have to be left to her friends, Ellie and Amy, to pick up the pieces — unless Nicola had left them flat to take up with Cadence. In any case, it wasn't Peri's problem. She just wished Nicola would take up with someone else.

Peri yawned and shifted the chewing gum into the other cheek. She half-hoped Ms Lancey would see it and order her out of assembly. Chewing gum was strictly forbidden on school premises, and wasn't that just like teachers? Hadn't they seen all the dental advertisements on TV that actually recommended the stuff to fight decay? They said parked chewies made too much of a mess of the paint work. It just went to show that to teachers, the paint work was more important than the students' teeth.

Mr Goodhew had come in, and was rambling on about the end of term, and how he hoped they'd all keep up the good work right to the end of the year. Peri yawned again, so widely her jaw muscles cracked. Then Ms Borrojavic got up on the dais.

Ms Borrojavic was still quite an unknown quantity because she had arrived halfway through the term as a replacement for the Speech and Drama teacher who had come down with some unspecified disease.

Little and slim and dark, Ms Borrojavic looked like you could blow her away with a drinking straw, but she'd basically decked some kid when he'd been acting big in Speech and Drama. Sure, she'd *said* she was teaching them to fall properly, but that had been some sort of judo throw or Peri was a monkey's uncle.

'I have an exciting project to put before you this morning,' Ms Borrojavic was saying in her clear, carrying voice, 'but before you all volunteer I must warn it will require considerable input from those who elect to be part of it. And I'm not just talking lunchtimes, either. This will mean staying back after school a couple of times a week and meeting through the holidays as well, right up until mid-February.'

'Yeah, right,' said someone from the front of the auditorium.

'Yeah, right!' said Ms Borrojavic. 'It will mean learning to work together as a team for some of you, and rehearsing in the summer holidays for others. Who wants in?'

Bazza Dudenski was the first to volunteer. 'Me!' he yelled from the front row. It was well-known that Bazza would volunteer for a dogfight, so there was a general groan. Then Cadence Merrick put up her hand. She *would*, thought Peri.

'Yes, Cadence?'

'I was wondering, Ms Borrojavic, if you could tell us a little more about it. I mean ...' and Cadence looked prettily earnest, 'if this is going to require a big commitment on our part, I think it's only fair that we know what we're in for. If you see what I mean?' She spread her hands and looked helplessly around the auditorium, inviting sympathy, and getting it. Cadence was as helpless as a spider at a convention of flies, Peri thought to herself.

'I see your point, Cadence,' said Ms Borrojavic crisply, 'but this is neither the time nor the place to go into the matter any further. All I can say at this point is those who think they might be interested in helping to write and produce an original piece of

musical theatre for the eisteddfod in February
should come to the library at lunchtime today. All
right?'

'Perfectly, thank you,' said Cadence. She smiled.
'You can rely on my cooperation in this, Ms
Borrojavic.'

Ms Borrojavic looked slightly stunned and Peri
snarled to herself. She parked her chewie under the
speaker again. Cadence Merrick was smarmy and it
was about time somebody did something about it.
Maybe — just maybe — Ms Borrojavic was the
woman to do it. And if Cadence was going to get
her comeuppance, Peri wanted to be there to see it
happen.

It was for that reason only that Peri went to the
meeting in the library. Most of the Year Ten Speech
and Drama kids were there, and a good sprinkling
from Years Nine and Eleven. Milling about like a
mob of sheep, thought Peri crossly. All hoping for a
bite at the cherry of stardom — well, she wasn't
going to hang on to Ms Borrojavic's words like the
others. She was only here to see Cadence Merrick
get hers.

'Shove over,' she said to a girl who took one
look at Peri's determined jaw and moved.

Ms Borrojavic had settled down in a chair,
leaving the rest of them to sit on the carpet or prop
themselves against the bookshelves. Dorky place to
hold a meeting, Peri thought. Libraries were for

reading and computers, not Speech and Drama, but at least Ms Borrojavic got right to the point.

'I don't know how many of you have heard of the eisteddfod. I gather it's something new for Longbeach, but perhaps some of you may have taken part in this sort of event somewhere else?'

There were a few doubtful nods and murmurs from the ballet brigade, and one or two sniggers from the boys.

'This year, the Drama Council has decided to sponsor an eisteddfod right here in Longbeach,' continued Ms Borrojavic. 'There will be a number of participants coming from outside the district, of course ...'

'Unfair! someone hissed.

'*But*,' Ms Borrojavic continued, 'although some of the companies in the musical play section may be much more experienced than you people, I have always believed that no-one can beat teenagers for enthusiasm and downright guts. Since the writing and production will take up a good deal of time, I must stress that this is for volunteers only, and I ask you to think carefully and sensibly about whether you wish to be involved.' She looked at them sternly, leaning forward as if she could see each face in the room and read the mind behind it. 'If we are to put up a creditable production you must be willing to give it every gram of your attention and commitment. I want no half-hearted performers. In short, I want you all to realise that it isn't just a chance to get into on-stage clinches with the hunkiest guys and coolest girls.'

'Of course not,' murmured a voice. Peri thought it was Cadence and scowled, an expression that came more naturally to her face than smiling.

'Yes — Peri Christian, isn't it?' Ms Borrojavic was looking straight at her.

'Nothing,' said Peri. 'I mean — you can count me out.' After all, Ms Borrojavic wasn't going to deal with Cadence — and if Cadence was *in*, Peri was *out*.

Ms Borrojavic nodded. 'Thank you for making yourself so clear so soon. Now, you and any other non-starters may leave so the rest of us can get down to business. Although — it is rather a pity. I would have thought a girl like you, Peri, would have benefited from this exercise.'

A girl like her! Peri knew what *that* meant. She was not on any sports teams, she did no community service work. She never joined any debates or went to any socials. Sometimes she wondered why she didn't; God knew she was bored enough most of the time. She supposed it boiled down to what old Goodhew called lack of motivation. She simply couldn't be bothered.

And there was Cadence Merrick sticking her hand in the air like they were still in Year Three, for

God's sake, and stupid little Nicola doing the same thing. Peri prepared to slouch out, but already there was a general move towards the door, so she hung back to let the crush go by. While she waited, Peri noticed something unpleasant about the exiting mob. They were all the wusses. Not the no-hopers — they hadn't come in the first place. Not the smartarses — they were staying. No, they were all the dorky ones who sat on the fence. They wanted to be part of the fun, but they didn't want the responsibility. Peri didn't like responsibility either, but she hated to ally herself to the wusses. And besides — Cadence was still acting the golden-haired girl. And Nicola would be bound to carry on about it all tonight. Peri decided to stay on for a bit — just to find out what she'd be missing.

CHAPTER 4

'It's going to be a *Rap Opera*! Isn't that excellent?' gushed Nicola.

'Original, anyway,' said Carolyn Christian cautiously.

'That's just what Ms Borrojavic said!' Nicola exclaimed.

God, did the girl have to look so starry-eyed? She was lit up like a Christmas tree and those big shiny eyes, plus the skinned-back hair, made her look exceedingly weird. Just like a bug-eyed alien.

'She said it was a *very* original idea and she'd never heard of anyone doing one before!' Nicola said.

'I wonder why that doesn't surprise me?' murmured Peter Christian, then answered his own question. 'Maybe because it's such terrible music?'

'Oh, I don't know,' said Mrs Christian consideringly. 'If Tom Jones can do it ...'

'Tom Jones! *Tom Jones*! Mum, where have you *been* the last ten years?'

There was no doubt about it — the bug-eyed alien was seriously over-excited. Peri rubbed Skates' soft black ears and shook her head.

'I've been bringing up you and Peri,' said Mrs Christian tartly, 'and a thankless job it is.'

'It was all Cadi's idea,' said Nicola adoringly. 'She always has the most excellent ideas.'

'Who's this Cadi?' asked her father. 'One of your teachers?'

'God, no — sorry Dad! I mean, she's Cadence Merrick, and she's in Year Ten.'

'Oh, one of the senior citizens.' Mr Christian winked at Peri, but she was concentrating on Skates.

'Is this a tick on his ear, d'you reckon?' she asked him.

Mr Christian put on his glasses to look. 'Just a mozzie bite, I reckon, but if you're worried put some powder on him.'

'Dogs don't get mozzie bites,' said Peri, and she went to get the tick powder.

'I wonder if she could be Rosina Merrick's daughter,' mused Mrs Christian. 'You know — she runs Sunnypots over at Sunnyside. Most of the Sunnyside kids go to Surfside High. She's got a boy, too — the same age as Duncan — Jason, remember? Nice boy, doing some sort of theatre course in Sydney.'

'Is he the one that used to go round with Linnet Valeria?' said Nicola.

'Probably. Is this girl, this Cadence, nice Nicky?'

'*Dad*!'

'I was only asking.'

'She's a smarmy little cow,' said Peri, 'always sucking up to the teachers.'

'She is not! Just because *you* don't like her — honestly, Dad, she doesn't suck up at all.'

'Pity,' murmured Mr Christian. 'A bit of kowtowing to authority is the sign of a healthy slave mentality — sorry — sorry. Don't kill me, Caro!'

'One more remark like that, old man, and you're on lawn-mowing detail for a month,' said Mrs Christian. 'Seriously, girls, what is this *Rap Opera* about?'

Peri sighed gustily, and sneezed as the tick powder rose in a cloud around her face. Here they went! She hadn't gone to the second meeting, but Nicola had, and she'd heard nothing but Cadence and *Rap Opera* ever since. Anyone would think the girl was going to produce the thing single-handed, instead of simply playing a small part.

'It's really rough on Cadi,' Nicola was saying earnestly. 'The *Rap Opera* was all her idea, but Ms Borrojavic says the people who write the script and the music can't have parts — not major parts, anyway.'

'Why's that?' asked Mrs Christian. 'Peri, *must* you do that in here?'

'Oh — you know,' said Nicola. 'She thinks it would be too much for them.'

'Bull,' said Peri, dusting her hands. 'She doesn't want your precious Cadence and her fan club writing plum parts to fit themselves. I mean — there're fifty kids breaking their necks to get a piece of the action, so why should five or six kids hog it all?'

'She did say she'd got the idea of this sort of team-writing from someone she used to teach with before she came here,' admitted Nicola. 'And apparently four Year Nines wrote the script of a musical and those four played the major parts. Some of the others got a bit annoyed about it.'

'So what's your friend Cadi going to do?' asked Mrs Christian.

'Brown-nose her way into doing both, I suppose,' said Peri sourly.

'No, she wants to act,' said Nicola, 'so she's stepped down from the script team.'

'She was never on it,' asserted Peri.

'You seem to know a good deal about this, Peri,' said her father. 'Dare we hope you're actually going to take part yourself?'

'Right, Dad, right. Joke over.'

'Why don't *you* try out for a part, Peri?' said Mrs Christian. 'You're quite musical.'

Yes, she was, and wasn't *that* a laugh? There was big brother Duncan the fledgling music teacher who was no relation to her at all, yet they could both sing. And there was the bug-eyed alien, who *was* related to Duncan, and she had a voice like a squeaky wheelbarrow.

'Nah — I'll be too busy,' she said.

'Doing what?' asked Mr Christian.

Peri looked up him from under her lashes, surprised at his tone.

'I repeat, doing *what*?' he said again.

Hanging around, that was what. Reading magazines, mooning over clothes she couldn't afford in Bojangles. Walking Skates and letting him go to the toilet on the letterboxes of people she didn't like. For a moment, she was almost tempted to give it a go. After all — what harm could it do her? And it might be okay to make a big success of a role in the *Rap Opera*. Yeah, she could make it a real triumph in February, and then old Borrojavic would weep tears of blood because the Julia Roberts of Surfside High was leaving school. She was tempted, really she was, but just as she drew breath to say nonchalantly that, what the heck, she might give it a go, Nicola broke in.

'Yes, *please* come in it with me, Peri. I really want you to, and so does Cadi. She thinks you'd be a real asset, with your voice. You wouldn't get the main part, of course, but there are plenty of others.'

That put a different complexion on the whole idea. 'Oh — piss off,' said Peri. 'Your hair looks so crappy, you may as well stick your head down the loo.'

That went down really well with the olds, of course. Mr Christian rapped his knife on the table and frowned at her, and Nicola went red and flounced off.

'It does look stupid,' said Peri, driven to defend herself. 'All smarmed down like that — her head looks like a pimple on a broom handle. And let's face it — her hair's the only asset she's got. For God's sake, she ought to be glad of a bit of advice.'

There was a nasty silence, and then Mrs Christian looked coldly at Peri. 'For what it's worth, Peri, I agree with you. Nicky's hair *does* look better tied back loosely. The thing is, she's at the right age for trying out new images for herself, and she'll probably be wearing it a different way next week, so it was pointlessly cruel of you to criticise her.'

'Is that so!' said Peri loudly. 'Then why wasn't it pointlessly cruel of you to criticise me when I had the extra holes put in my ears? *Cheap*, you said, and *common*! But of course that doesn't matter, does it. I'm only Peri, the bottom of the heap. Little Nicky's the star of *this* family.' She gave an outraged sob, which was only half for effect, and pushed back her chair. 'I'm going to bed!' she said loudly.

'Come back here, Peri and finish your meal,' said Mr Christian. 'You know your mother didn't mean it like that.'

'She's not my bloody mother!' howled Peri, and screeched back her chair, scaring Skates into a yip of surprise.

This time, they let her go.

CHAPTER
5 five

Nicola wasn't part of the script-writing team, and although she went to the audition in the holidays, she wasn't picked for a part in the opera.

'No wonder,' said Peri to Skates. 'She's too bloody meek to be a rapper.' Sometimes she wished she could talk to someone other than Skates, but at least Skates didn't call her *pointlessly cruel* when she ventured an opinion.

If the opera hadn't been Cadence Merrick's baby, Peri might still have been tempted to audition herself. She rather fancied herself as a rapper, all smouldering eyes and husky, driving rhythm. She couldn't see Cadence being much good, but sure enough, Cadence got the chief part.

'She's playing Rapture Red!' said Nicola, almost swooning with excitement. 'Cass Tranton thought she was a shoo-in to get it, but Cadi's playing it after all.'

'Pity,' said Peri, who didn't mind Cass Tranton. 'And who's Rapture Red when she's at home? A porn queen?'

'Don't be a dweeb, Peri.'

Oh, so Peri was a dweeb now? Who cared for the opinions of bug-eyed aliens, anyway?

'Rapture Red and The Miner are the main parts. See, it all takes place on the streets — only it's in the future, after World War Three,' Nicola gushed.

'If there's a World War Three, we'd all be nuked,' said Peri. 'There won't be any streets left, let alone any rapture. And miners are exploiting the planet.'

'There's a future, in the musical,' said Nicola firmly. 'And everyone over about twenty-one is dead —'

'Sounds like an old sci-fi film,' said Peri.

'And everyone left has turned themselves into tribes —'

'Sounds like *Mad Max*.'

'And the teenagers have built their own society —'

'Sounds like *Lord of the Flies*.'

'*And*,' said Nicola loudly, 'Rapture Red, this gorgeous eighteen year old —'

'Who's never gonna make old bones ...'

'— has to choose her man.'

'Oooh, caaarry me out and laaay me dowownnn!' said Peri, and swooned across the couch. 'So,' she said, sitting up again, 'who's the unlucky bloke?'

There was a pause. 'Adam Primrose,' Nicola said in a muffled voice. She got suddenly very busy studying a spot on the carpet.

Peri smiled sourly. If Cadence Merrick had a male counterpart, it was Adam Primrose, silver-spoon kids, both of them. But Peri couldn't see Adam rapping either. 'What will they be wearing?' she asked idly.

'Rapture's wearing red vinyl — skin-tight, with a red wig. The Miner's in black. Ivory and Goldcoast and Teak are ...'

'Don't tell me — white, yellow and brown. Now ask me how I guessed — go on!'

'I'd have thought it was obvious,' said Nicola.

'It is. So why tell me?'

'I didn't.'

'Oh, but you would've,' said Peri, 'if I hadn't got in first.'

There was a pause, and she could see Nicola's lips moving as she worked that one out. She sighed. It wasn't much fun winding Nicola up. It was too pitifully easy. If only the kid had a bit more bite she'd have been halfway okay.

'I wish I could have been in it,' said Nicola wistfully. 'It would have been really cool — but at least I can help with the sets and that.'

Big deal, thought Peri, but didn't say it. Old Carolyn's words — *pointlessly cruel* — had stuck in her mind.

'Why don't you help out, too?' asked Nicola. 'There's heaps to do — all the costumes to make and backdrops to be painted. And all the choreography has to be worked out still. Do you reckon Duncan would help out on the musical side if we asked him especially?'

'How the heck should I know? You ask him — he's your brother.'

'I might then,' said Nicola. 'After all, he's coming up at Christmas with Debbie — maybe she'll help out, too!'

For Peri the disadvantages of having a stepbrother who was musical were legion. For a start, Duncan hated to see talent going to waste, and he was always on at Peri to do something with her voice. 'Good altos don't grow on trees, Fairy,' he said far too often. 'You owe it to yourself to get some training.'

The irony was that if Duncan hadn't kept on about it, Peri might have thought about it. There were plenty of musical groups at school, but Peri wasn't into groups, and she couldn't do much on her own. And calling her 'Fairy', for God's sake! Just because a peri was a Persian elf didn't give him the right to be funny at her expense.

Duncan had tried to give her some training himself, once. What a fiasco! Peri'd ended up screaming at him so much Mrs Christian had made Duncan leave her alone.

The other disadvantage was that school teachers had almost as much holiday time as students — and at the same time. So Duncan was going to be able to come up the coast in December and infest Longbeach. And he'd be bringing his girlfriend, a dork called Debbie. Debbie was blonde and blue-eyed with pouty lips and daggy clothes. She was a very serious singer, and was always doing breathing exercises and playing scales, and trying to get Peri to sing duets.

'At least,' said Peri, 'if you can talk those two into helping out with your *Rap Opera* it might stop them hanging around here, using the place like a hotel.'

'Peri — that was uncalled for,' said Mr Christian. 'Duncan has as much right to spend as much time here as you do.'

Peri stomped out. They were into fourth term and the sparklers in her head were getting worse. She didn't really want to be angry all the time, but sometimes it seemed she just couldn't bear anyone near her. Not her father or stepmother, because they were trying to organise her life. Not Nicola, because she was such a wuss. Not the loudmouths at school, and not the achievers either — God, if only she had someone other than Skates that she could really talk to! Someone who would see through the spikes and the bad-mouthing to the real Peri underneath. If there *was* a real Peri underneath. Sometimes, she wondered about that.

Pointlessly cruel. Peri didn't want to be pointlessly cruel, but so often the things that sounded like smart ripostes in her mind came out as rude put-downs.

'You like me, don't you Skates?' she said aloud. Skates beamed up at her and wagged his stump. Skates liked her a lot, but he was a dog, after all, and what dog wouldn't like a bitch?

CHAPTER 6
six six

Nicola went to watch all the rehearsals of the *Rap Opera*. Peri kept seeing her in the corridors at school, clutching a script and looking important, or scribbling notes on a clipboard.

'You've only got to shift a few bits of furniture,' said Peri in disgust. 'Don't pretend to be so busy!'

'I have to know what's going on,' said Nicola defensively. 'I'm understudy prompt.'

'Really.'

'I mean, I'm sitting in the wings following the script so if someone forgets his or her words and the prompt is away, I can cue him or her in. That means I have a microphone and ...'

Peri rounded in on her ferociously. 'For God's sake! I *know* what that means, you cretin! Why do you always sound so bloody *stupid*?' She clenched her hands, suddenly frightened. She could easily have hit Nicola then. Or done *anything* to her, just so long as she stopped rabbiting on and shut up!

People were staring, so Peri flung away and went to the girls' toilet. There were the usual hand-washers, loiterers, gossips and nail-polishers in there, but Peri slammed into a stall and flushed the water repeatedly. She heard the siren sound for the end of lunch, but she ignored it, made a cushion of torn up loo-paper and sat down on the lid of the toilet. She found she was breathing too fast — hyperventilating, it was called — and there was a reddish mist behind her eyes. She was shaking, and felt slightly sick. God, she could have hit Nicola, and for what? For being her usual younger-sisterly, bug-eyed alien self! So she'd said something stupid. A kid ought to be able to say stupid things to a sister — even a half-sister — without getting herself strangled. These rages Peri got into — surely they weren't normal? Did other people see the world through a series of angry, fizzing sparks? Did other people find their relatives and fellow students horribly, unbearably irritating? And it wasn't just her family and fellow students — it was everyone. Everywhere Peri went there was someone to annoy her.

Slowly, Peri fought herself back to control. If this went on much longer, someone would notice and send her to a shrink. They'd haul her off and start poking and prying, running tests on hormone levels and blood counts to see if they could find out what was bugging her. Before Peri let that happen she'd have to do a bit of investigating herself.

'Think, Peri,' she muttered aloud. 'Use that famous brain of yours. What makes your time bomb tick? Why did you want to hit poor old alien Nickers? Not just because she's stupid — Skates isn't a genius and you'd never hit him.'

So what set her off into these fizzing irritations, what touched off the sudden surges of rage? The answer came back pat — everyone. Not animals, not dear old Skates, even when he scratched under her bed at night. It was *people* she couldn't stand, prying, interfering, organising, yakking, gushing, ordering people. Too bad she couldn't be a hermit.

Then there was the feeling of having too much to do but still being bored. Never a moment alone, yet no-one interesting to talk to. Heaps of people ordering her around, no-one treating her seriously as an intelligent person, capable of making her own choices. To everyone else she was just sulky Peri Christian, the odd one out in the pleasant Christian family. A real no-hoper.

But Peri knew she was more than that. The sum of parts simply didn't add up to the whole. If only she could find someone she liked, really liked, she'd be a good friend. If Skates could talk he'd vouch for that. If only she could find something she was good at and enjoyed, she'd apply herself. If only someone would give her a chance to be herself and then stand back and leave her be — oh, then she'd show them! Then she'd show them all.

But that was just wishful thinking.

So Peri decided she'd stop looking at what made her mad and think about what made her feel good instead. The answer to that was brief. Precious little. She liked drawing designs, she liked playing with her dog. She liked sounds — water splashing into the bath, the rush of rain on the roof ...

Peri blew her nose, suddenly aware that she had been shedding a few tears of self-pity.

'Look at you,' she mocked herself, 'sitting on a toilet lid bawling!' She could feel herself uncurling, unclenching inside, and then she noticed the quiet. It was quiet in the toilets, now the siren had gone. Sure, there was the soft hum of the air conditioning, and there was a distant buzz of talk and work and a teacher was clacking down past the door, but compared to the way it had been in the corridor ten minutes before, it was as silent as a tomb.

She thought back. The last time she had felt really relaxed had been when she had had the house to herself, way back last term!

So *that* was it! She needed some time to herself. She needed time in her own company to see if she liked herself. There was no way of being alone at home — someone else was nearly always home, and the summer holidays would be worse, what with Duncan and Debbie and sometimes Jo infesting the place. Even in term time, Nicola was always there, pottering about humming or singing, and Carolyn was always listening to the radio. Or the TV was on while Peri's dad soaked up the news.

School was impossibly noisy, unless you hung out in the loo as she was doing now, and it was no good going to Coco's, the coffee shop, or Guiseppe's — they were the noisiest places of all. There was always the beach, but that was full of surfers and swimmers, not to say the dorks who still sunbaked, courting melanomas.

Peri decided she'd have to find a place for herself, a place no-one else would go, and try to spend a few hours there each week. Alone. And see if that did any good. Otherwise, she'd turn into a screaming raving loony, and would probably end up doing something stupid. Probably to Nicola. Or her stepmother. Or Cadence Merrick. And that wouldn't look too good on her résumé, would it?

Peri came cautiously out of the loo as the siren went for the next period and blended into the rushing tide of kids. It was noisy, but now Peri had something to hang on to she could try being more human, just in case it might get to be a habit.

With this in mind, Peri cornered Nicola when they got home from school.

'What do you want?' Nicola asked distrustfully.

'C'mon, I'm going to give you a new look,' said Peri. 'That hair's a disaster.'

Nicola clasped her hands protectively over her skinned-back hair. 'You're not cutting my hair.'

'Don't go ballistic! There's a lot you can do with styling wands and clips.'

Peri directed a protesting Nicola into the bathroom and pressed her onto a stool. 'Sit down and shut up,' she said smiling. She plugged in the wand, seized a comb and hauled the scrunchie out of Nicola's hair.

'Ouch! *Peri*!'

'Don't be a wuss.'

Energetically, Peri combed out Nicola's kinking curls. She used the wand to create some soft wispy spirals around Nicola's face and then swept back the rest and tied it with a large soft scarf. 'There!'

Nicola looked doubtfully at her reflection. 'Gee, Peri — I look older, don't you reckon?'

'You look *better* anyway,' said Peri.

She felt surprisingly good about Nicola's transformation — a feeling that remained until dinnertime when she noticed Nicola had scraped back her hair, back into the scrunchie.

'It kept getting in my eyes,' said Nicola defensively.

'So the bug-eyed alien returns. Jeez, why did I even bother?' snarled Peri. Again her hands itched to shake Nicola but she took Skates for a walk instead. 'Guess I really need that quiet place, mate!' she said, and Skates grinned up at her and snorted agreement.

Peri found her quiet place in the rainforest that ran up from the beach. It was beautiful in a rather threatening way, with all sorts of stinging, prickling plants and a lot of leeches and insects that just lived to suck your blood. Peri was no naturalist, but she knew the rainforest at this time of year would be practically deserted. Later, after Christmas, the summer people would arrive. There would be a rash of accidents as they tried to swim where they shouldn't, surf where they couldn't, rough up the local guys and crack onto the local girls. Some of them would get stung by jellyfish, some would get heatstroke or sunburn or break their toes kicking the rocks. Some of them would leave their food out in the sun and get salmonella poisoning and try to blame the local shopping centre. And a lot of them would get badly stung and scratched trying to force their way through the rainforest to the waterfall.

But for now, the rainforest was quiet.

Peri made her first getaway on day six of the school cycle. Day six was a nothing day, double Art, double PE, Speech and Drama, Home Ec and Japanese. Missing any of that lot was nothing to cry about. If her teachers noticed she wasn't there, they'd probably be glad.

Peri got on the bus with Nicola as usual, but at the stop closest to the beach she suddenly got up and pushed her way to the door. 'Gotta go and get something!' she yelled to Nicola, and jumped out before the bug-eyed alien could say anything. If she even noticed. She was jabbering twenty-five to the dozen at Cadence Merrick.

Peri watched the bus roar away. She wished she had Skates with her but there was no way she could have smuggled him on board the school bus. She hauled on the knapsack she used as a school bag, and walked until she was hidden from the road and the beach. Then she took off her tights and skirt and pulled on a pair of old shorts and some long hiking socks that belonged to her father. The polo shirt would do — she repacked her bag, with her school lunch and extra drink, and set off along the track.

The rainforest was steamy and green and Peri was careful to stick to the mathematical centre of the track. There was no way she was going to get herself all swelled up but just in case she *did* happen to brush against something nasty, she had taken a tube of antihistamine cream from the bathroom cabinet. And just in case she *met* anything nasty, she had the bottle of spray-on dye her stepmother had forced her to carry a few weeks before.

Peri walked for twenty minutes, carefully side-stepping a lush green stinging tree, then stopped to get her bearings. If she remembered rightly, there should be another little track branching off. It led down to a pool, with a basalt shelf sloping right down to the edge of the water.

The little track was there — just — but it was obvious it hadn't been used since last summer. Tendrils of vine and bramble grew across the opening and Peri looked at it hard. Then she picked up two stout sticks and used them like salad tongs to manoeuvre the vines out of the way. It was slow going, but the branch-track was short, and in about ten minutes she had ducked round another lush stinging tree and reached the little pool she remembered.

She stopped and looked about with satisfaction. There was a small waterfall, and the few old chip packets and empty cans were so old and battered they practically counted as historic relics. Peri sat down on the sun-warmed basalt and leaned back contentedly. It was so quiet. She had intended to brood about her problems, perhaps to even cry a little, but bit by bit peace stole over her and soaked into her bones. She watched the little waterfall and felt happy. It was so long since she'd felt this good. It was absolutely wonderful.

At midday, she ate her lunch. She would have liked to have stripped off and swum in the little pool but swimming alone wasn't such a clever idea. She pottered about and watched the scrub wrens, and the patterns the leaves made in the sun, and the dimples on the water. She sketched designs for some really wild party gear and added some gumleaf inspired jewellery. And after a while, lulled by the splash of the water and the murmur of the trees, she went to sleep.

She woke a couple of hours later, warm and relaxed and full of well-being. All the sparklers in her head seemed to have sputtered out, and she could see quite clearly what had been wrong.

'Sensory overload,' she said aloud. They were the first words she had heard spoken since she had yelled at Nicola as she escaped from the bus. And why not? Whoever said human beings had to jabber at one another all the time? She glanced at her watch. School would be out in another half-hour — she hadn't really intended to stay so long. But even if she was late home, even if she got blasted for this, even though she knew she would never make or wear that party gear, it would still have been worth it.

Reluctantly, she packed up her belongings, the sketch pad and the unused Walkman, and hiked back through the rainforest. She hesitated about putting her tights and skirt back on, but in the end decided not to bother; with luck she would get home before Nicola or Carolyn and her dad.

Peri made it, too, had a shower, and put her socks in the wash. She caught sight of her face in the steamy bathroom mirror and stared at it for a moment. It didn't look like her at all. It looked somehow serene ...

Peri was stretched out on the couch when Nicola came home. She was obviously wondering where Peri had got to, but she didn't ask. And that suited Peri just fine. Not that she'd have minded Nicola knowing, exactly, but she didn't feel like sharing her experience just yet. Nicola might have wanted to come, too.

CHAPTER 7 seven

Peri was much too smart to go to the pool, her private place, very often, but she usually made it at least once a week — sometimes twice. Mostly she went there on the weekends, occasionally she took a day or a half-day off school, but she picked them at random so there would be no identifiable pattern.

Strangely, even the thought of her private place could calm her at times — Peri could think ahead and promise herself a visit there where she could sit in the quiet for two or three hours and draw and nobody would bug her at all. On the first day of the summer holidays, she took Skates with her, taking the long way round, through the main street of Longbeach. She stopped off at the newsagent's to flick through the latest magazines, thinking she might take one with her and read for a change. *'Natural Beauties'*, said the cover teaser of the top one, Peri put it aside. Natural beauties were pale and lipless. '*Legendary Lovelies,*' said the next.

That was more like it, and she gazed at Greta Garbo, Queen Nefertiti, Clara Bow and Elizabeth Taylor as Cleopatra. A flat stick of kohl slid from a plastic pocket slotted between the pages and Peri picked it up. '*Now you too may ... (continued on page 16),*' she read.

Peri turned curiously to page 16. The woman at the counter, Ma Banks, gave her a disapproving look and sighed deeply. As if reading a magazine would wear out the print for anyone else! Stubbornly Peri read to the end of the article, but Ma Banks' eyes seemed to be drilling little holes in her shoulder blades, so Peri flung the magazine back onto the stack, jammed her hands into her pockets and slouched out. She'd lost interest in reading.

'Rotten shop — won't even let dogs in,' she remarked as she unhitched Skates from the rail outside. He leapt up to push a cold nose against her elbow.

They were halfway down the street, heading for the rainforest, when Peri felt a warning prickle in her nose. She hauled out her handkerchief and fielded the sneeze, then glanced around to make sure no-one had heard. There was something ridiculous about sneezing in public. It wasn't quite as bad as hiccuping, but several degrees worse than belching, because that at least could be voluntary. She didn't know anyone who could sneeze to order, although there were several accomplished farters at school. Peri blew her nose and, as she put away the handkerchief, her fingers touched something slim and hard in her pocket. It felt like a stick of chewing gum, maybe the last of a highly-scented kind she had bought to annoy her stepmother. She scowled at the thought. Last night the question of Year Eleven versus freedom had raged, with Peri on one side, Carolyn on the other and her dad hovering uneasily in between. Peri had used some of her newly-won calm to force herself to talk to them quietly instead of screaming, but she hadn't really got anywhere. The only concession she had wrung out of them was that if she managed to find a full-time, permanent-type job during the next two months she could take it on and leave school. And the chances of *that* were about as good as the chances of finding a nice crop of hens' teeth. So it looked like come February, Peri'd be in a good position to check for her chewie under the speaker and see if she'd won her bet.

Peri drew out the thin packet. It wasn't gum after all, but the kohl stick from the magazine. She must have stuck it into her pocket when she'd picked it up. She hadn't meant to nick it, but she wasn't about to sneak back to the shop now. Might as well put it to good use. She patted the back pocket of her black jeans to check for the comb and compact mirror she kept there. All present and correct.

It was a treat walking through the greenery with Skates. Just as well Peri had him on the leash, because he sniffed and woofed happily in all directions and it was obvious he'd have liked to have gone off hunting the rustles and squeaks in the undergrowth. The excitement of the rainforest tired him out, so by the time they reached the pool, Skates was ready to lie down to snooze in the shade while Peri settled on her usual basalt shelf. The rock was pleasantly warm, as it nearly always was, and the sun struck down through her shirt. It was one she had designed and made herself in Home Ec, one of the few things she had ever produced that had almost satisfied her.

The shirt was made of black stretch cotton with a bold appliqué design in ochre and green. Of course it was a bit of a waste to wear it down at the pool where no-one would ever see her, but it made sense to wear her favourite things to her favourite place with her favourite person (or dog) for company.

She wiggled her mirror out of her pocket and set it on the rock. She sat down, planted her booted feet on either side of the mirror, and leaned over. Her face looked back at her, pale and still sulky from last night's argument with her dad and stepmother. Peri bit her lips to redden them, rubbed furiously at her cheekbones with her fists and then, steadying her elbows on her knees, began to outline her eyes with kohl.

Elizabeth Taylor as Cleopatra — *Peri Christian as who?* Peri couldn't recall any famous beauties with long crinkly brown hair, narrow dark eyes and high cheekbones like hers.

Approaching noises interrupted her musing and she looked up in disgust. Crunching feet, slashing sticks, a mutter of voices as well.

'Damn!' she said. This was her place, her private place, and she didn't want to be interrupted. She didn't want people knowing she came here and she didn't want any hassles. And if some of those summer guys from last year found her here, there *would* be hassles. She might even be driven to using the spray-on dye to change the colours of their day.

Skates cocked his ears and growled. Peri hushed him and gathered up his leash, looking about for the best avenue of escape. Unfortunately, there didn't seem to be one, unless she felt like plunging off into a thicket of spiteful thorns and other nasties. Damn, she thought, but she wasn't going to be caught cringing like a scared wuss, either. She was damned well going to sit here as if she owned the place. Which she felt she did.

Incredibly, the feet stopped crunching, the sticks stopped slashing, and the muttering voices became raised in argument.

Peri held her breath. Maybe whoever it was would turn back! She was always careful not to slash down the vegetation herself, not because she particularly minded knocking down a few bits of rainforest, but because she had wanted to keep the place as private as possible. If she *had* made a beaten track, the dweebs or surfies would use it. There was a particularly nasty stinging bush just before you got to the clearing — she banked on that to keep any but the thickest-skinned away.

'Go back,' she mouthed, soothing Skates and giving the exit from the grove the evil eye. 'Go back. There's nothing here at all. Nothing. Go back.'

She listened closely and realised that not only were the voices both female, which she hadn't somehow expected, but that she recognised one of them. Cadence Merrick. God! If there was one person she didn't want barging in on her, it was Cadence. If Cadence came in, the whole place would be spoiled, polluted by her presence, and Peri wouldn't come back ever.

There was another burst of argument from beyond the stinging tree.

'Look, we can't possibly do it now. I'm coming up in a whole lot of red lumps. I'll look ugly. Let's get back to the beach.' Cadence, the cow, and she'd obviously had a close encounter with the stinging tree. 'Ow! It burns — I've got to get back to my bag and put something on it!'

'Oh — all *right*! I'm going on, but I won't be long.' That was the other voice, and it sounded as exasperated as Peri always did when confronted with Cadence.

'It isn't any good — you might as well come straight back with me. You don't want a stinging tree on a calendar.'

'I can tell you what I *don't* want, and that's a bathing beauty. That's been done to death.'

'So have girly calendars.'

There was a loud sigh, then the second voice said, very quietly, 'Give me strength! This is not a bloody girly calendar! God, if Victoria hadn't started puking up I wouldn't be bothering with you now. If I could have got hold of someone else, believe me, I would, but I couldn't use professionals and most of the girls I know have taken off to Greece or the Gold Coast for their holidays. If it wasn't for this bloody play of Merrick's, I'd have pissed off, too. Oh — go on, get your bag. I'll push on to the pool for a look, then come back for you.'

There was an angry swish and a yell from Cadence.

The stinging tree strikes again, thought Peri with satisfaction, and she hoped the other girl, whoever she was, would give up too. She sounded a bit strange, anyway, talking about girls, professionals — not to speak of girly calendars ... Peri's thoughts snapped off as a branch of the stinging tree swung down and away and a young woman entered the grove, backwards. She was tall and what magazines call willowy, and when she turned round Peri saw that she had long red hair, green sunglasses and clear, unfreckled skin. She looked to be at least twenty-one, and she was carrying a large bulky bag, an aluminium tripod and a technical-looking camera. 'I knew I wasn't wrong!' she said with obvious satisfaction.

Peri stared. The woman hadn't seen her yet, and was scrabbling round in the bag, setting up the tripod and waving a soft cloth about, flicking dust off a lens shaped like a pig's snout. The quick, whisking movements were familiar, ringing all sorts of bells although surely ...

'Well, well!' whispered Peri to Skates. 'That's just got to be Linnet Valeria. I wonder what *she's* doing back in town?'

Linnet Valeria had been in Year Ten when Peri had started at Surfside High. Usually, the Year Sevens hardly knew any of the Year Tens — the gap between eleven and fifteen was wider than Bass Strait. But Linnet Valeria had been special, like a comet that flashed through the school, red hair bouncing, temper spurting. She had been part of everything — Camera Club, Sports Club, Car Club, Debating Club — by the look of that camera equipment, she'd kept up at least one of those interests. Peri remembered that she'd been part of a foursome which had included her own stepbrother Duncan, dull Debbie, and — who was the other guy?

Ah, yes — *Merrick*. Cadence Merrick's brother, but nothing like Cadence. A thin dark boy with bright eyes and quicksilver movements to match Linnet's.

Peri had thought Linnet was great then, and had never understood why Duncan had taken up with Debbie instead. She didn't know her now though, and the woman was invading her own private place. *And* she'd been about to drag Cadence into it — still might, if Peri couldn't dissuade her. Deliberately, she released Skates, who dashed up and jammed his cold nose against Linnet Valeria's thigh.

'Bloody hell!' Linnet pushed Skates away, then, spotting Peri, slowly removed her sunglasses. Her eyes were bright green, just as Peri remembered. 'Well, well, well!' said Linnet slowly. 'If it isn't the fairy!'

Peri frowned and snapped her fingers for Skates.

Linnet laughed. 'Well?' she prompted. '*Aren't* you Dunnycan Graham's kid sister?'

'No,' said Peri coldly. 'That's Nicola. I'm no relation to him at all. Thank God.'

Linnet nodded. 'I take it he hasn't improved, then,' she said cheerfully. 'He was always a bit of a dweeb.'

'You can say that again.'

'I haven't seen him yet,' said Linnet reflectively. 'But we've only been back five minutes.'

'*We*?'

'Merrick brought me up to Longbeach,' said Linnet, 'on the back of his God-awful bike. Never

again, I told him, and this time I mean it! I'm
renting a car while I'm here.'

Merrick? So Cadence Merrick's big brother was
back, too.

'That explains what you were doing with creepy
Cadence,' said Peri. 'Keeping in with her big brother.'

'Bull.' Linnet stopped messing about with the
camera and sat down on the rock next to Peri,
giving Skates a wary look. 'Does that dog bite?'

'Sic her, Skates!' said Peri ferociously. 'Trouble!'

Skates barked and bounced then yawned and sat
down. Linnet laughed.

'That's my answer, I take it. Right. I'm only
hanging round with Cadi because I'm bloody
desperate.'

'You must be,' Peri retorted.

'Desperate for a model,' said Linnet austerely.
'Look, I'm working on a calendar shoot for a big
competition. My friend Victoria Southey has a sort
of models' agency, so there shouldn't have been
any trouble getting bodies to pose, but one of the
rules is that the subjects can't have earned money
as a model. That wipes out all of Tory's girls, but
not Tory herself, oddly enough. So I had old Tory
all lined up to pose as Ms December, and what does
she do? Gets herself pregnant. Hey — I don't care
if she's pregnant or not — it'd be a nice angle,
actually — but man, like, she's *green*!'

'Yeah?' said Peri.

'So it boiled down to Cadence,' said Linnet, 'seeing there's not a lot left of December.'

'That doesn't matter, does it?' Peri asked.

'It's in the rules, kid,' said Linnet. 'The entries have to have been taken within the last year, and the closing date is January the second. I meant to get cracking ages ago, but Merrick hauled me back here for the holidays and I've left it all to the last minute, like the cretin I am.'

'So?' said Peri.

'So, I'm stuck with Cadi-wadi.' Linnet shoved her fingers through her hair and flung out her arms. 'Why me, God?' she yelled, making Skates jump up excitedly. 'Why *me*? Listen, kid, if it wasn't for bloody Tory, I could have used myself for a model! Thing is, she got me a bit of work in a lingerie ad, two years back, and I got paid. Damn!'

'Do you do this all the time?' asked Peri.

'What? Sit bitching on a rock in the rainforest?'

'I mean, are you a photographer?'

'Yeah, for my sins. I do pics for catalogues, adverts, portraits, weddings — sometimes calendars. You name it, I click it.' She picked up the camera and turned its pig-snout on Peri. 'Like that.' Click! There was a little pause.

'I didn't say you could take my photograph!' said Peri, annoyed.

Linnet shrugged. 'So sue me. Hey — you've never worked as a model, have you, Fairy?'

'Peri.'

'Peri. Right. Have you?'

'No.'

'Never been Miss Showgirl or Miss Longbeach? Never been Miss Guiseppe's Pizzas?'

Peri shook her head in disgust.

'Good,' said Linnet. 'Then you just got yourself nominated. You're Ms December and I'm saved from Cadi-wadi.' She paused. 'Aren't you going to say something?'

'Yeah,' said Peri. 'I think I'm gonna spew.'

'Hey,' said Linnet, 'what have you got against being photographed?'

Nothing. Peri had nothing against being photographed. What she didn't like was being press-ganged like this. And being chosen just because there was nobody else — aside from Cadence Merrick. If Cadence had been the apple on the bottom of the barrel, what was Peri? The apple that had rolled *under* the barrel? For the first time at the grove by the pool, she felt the sparklers of rage beginning to fizz. That made her madder still. Bloody Linnet, swanning in here and taking over.

'Look,' Peri said coldly, 'I came here for some peace. Okay? I am not interested in making myself pretty-pretty for a calendar. Get it?'

'No? Then what were you doing with that?' Linnet pointed to the mirror and the stick of kohl.

'And why are you dressed like that? Hey — you're not waiting for your boyfriend, are you?'

'Gimme a break!'

'Why are you so pissed off then?'

'Because this is my place and you've come barging in. I'm going home!'

Linnet laughed. 'Sorry for breathing! But honestly, Peri, I used to come here when I was a kid. It is pretty special, isn't it? That's why I wanted to do the shoot here. Cadence, of course, thinks it ought to be down on the beach.'

'She would.'

'Cadence,' said Linnet, 'just wants to be seen to be being photographed. Look,' she added persuasively, 'why not let me take a few shots of you anyway, and then we'll call it quits. I'll find Cadence and leave you alone. I'll tell her I couldn't find the place, or it was too hard, or something. Deal?'

'Deal,' said Peri. Anything was better than having Cadence charging in and posing all over the place. 'Skates can be in the pictures, too.'

'He's too ugly,' said Linnet.

Peri stuck out her jaw. 'No Skates, no pics. And I won't look pretty-pretty.'

'Don't worry — you couldn't if you tried.'

CHAPTER 8
eight

Christmas was Christmas. Peri could have done without it this year. Her dad and Carolyn were still chilly about her leaving school and Nicola was lit up about the cruddy eisteddfod. Worst of all, Duncan and dull Debbie came to stay.

Duncan hadn't landed a job for the new year and he was very cut up about it. Debbie kept on trying to cheer him up, and that made Peri feel mildly ill. If Duncan wanted to sulk, let him! But no — Debbie couldn't leave well alone. 'After all, you did really well in your prac,' she kept saying. 'It's not as if you won't have that to put on your résumé.'

'Prac!' said Duncan. 'God! All they'll be able to think about is why am I still available?'

'Because of staff cuts,' said Debbie helpfully.

'*I* know that, *you* know that, but they'll just want to know why it was me that got left out and not the other sixteen point-five teachers.'

Peri chewed her lip, wondering how you could have point-five of a teacher. Did the left side come to work, or just the right? Or did they get the chop at waist level? She could think of quite a few teachers *she* wouldn't mind seeing on the chopping block.

Duncan sighed, and turned to Peri. 'Look, Peri — Dad says you're thinking about leaving school. That isn't true — is it?'

'Why shouldn't I?' asked Peri defensively.

'Your job prospects are ever so much better if you stay on,' put in Debbie.

'I see!' said Peri. 'If I stay on being bored to death for two more years I, too, can have the pleasure of being "available".'

'Peri! That's enough,' said Mr Christian. 'You have no right to make judgements about your brother's work.'

'*Step*brother!' hissed Peri. 'And why not? He was sticking his nose pretty freely into *my* affairs.'

'Duncan is concerned about your future, Peri,' said Mrs Christian. 'None of us wants you to end up without qualifications or a job, simply because you're not motivated enough to make use of the brains you undoubtedly have.'

'*He* has qualifications and what good's that done him? On the scrap heap before he even gets started!'

Obviously Mr Christian thought the discussion had gone far enough, for he changed the subject. 'A few weeks ago you two mentioned you were auditioning for parts in the *Messiah*,' he said to his stepson. 'Did anything ever come of it?'

Debbie went pink, and glanced at Duncan. There was a nasty silence, and Peri pricked up her ears.

'Debbie's the soprano soloist,' said Duncan.

'And Dunc's down as a possible to understudy the tenor,' put in Debbie hastily.

'Only if Richard Farr can't do it, and it's pretty certain he can,' Duncan reminded her.

Peri looked at them covertly and thought how alike they were with their fair hair and blue eyes. Almost like brother and sister. Practically incest. And all this mutual admiration and support! Give them a few years and they'd be married with two point five kids and calling one another 'Mummy' and 'Daddy'.

'I hope you get it,' Nicola said.

Peri sniffed. The bug-eyed alien was keeping in with the wrinklies. Again. And, whatever her stepmother said, the stupid dweeb was still skinning her hair back. She'd been under Cadence Merrick's thumb for practically three months — if she didn't get out soon, she'd become a permanent carbon Cadi-copy. Pity. She'd looked halfway okay when Peri had done her hair for her.

'I've already said I'm quite willing to drop out if you don't get a part,' Debbie was saying. Which was just like dull Debbie.

'Don't be silly, Debs. It's a chance that doesn't come along every day, and if it doesn't come off for me that's cool. I'm going to be fully occupied looking for a job. Or giving Merrick a hand with his show.'

Just like Saint Duncan, Peri thought.

'Oh, but we want you to help with the *Rap Opera*!' broke in the bug-eyed alien. 'Cadi says ...'

Duncan smiled at her. 'I'm surprised young Cadence isn't auditioning for her brother's play!' he said. 'It's bound to be a lot more professional than a school musical.'

'It hardly seems fair that the kids have to compete with adults who are being directed by a professional,' said Mrs Christian. 'Surely there should be sections according to age!'

'Actually,' said Duncan, 'I'm surprised to find this happening at Longbeach at all.'

'We're such a backwater here, aren't we?' said Peri. Then she added, 'I suppose it's too much to ask what you're all going on about?'

'If you'd listen instead of sulking, you'd know,' said Mrs Christian crisply.

Peri's anger surfaced. 'If nobody wants to fill me in, I'm off to bed.'

'Don't be like that, Fairy,' said Duncan.

If he called her that one more time, she'd hit him one and damn the consequences!

But Debbie was rushing to fill the gap, just as

she always did. 'It's quite simple, Peri. Have you heard of Longbeach Rep?'

'Sort of,' said Peri vaguely. 'They're a bunch of wrinklies who do plays in winter. Shakespeare, and that, with Romeo about fifty-five not out and Juliet a toothy forty.'

'They've decided to enter a musical in the eisteddfod, and they're getting in a directing student from Sydney — you remember Dunc's friend, Merrick?'

'Cadi's brother,' put in Nicola helpfully. 'His real name's Jason, but he doesn't like it, Cadi says, because ...'

Peri yawned, and abruptly lost interest. So Linnet Valeria's old boyfriend was going to be directing wrinklies in a musical. So what? She yawned loudly. 'I'm taking Skates for a walk and then I'm going to bed.'

CHAPTER 9

On Boxing Day, the bug-eyed alien was all lit up —
again. 'Guess what?' she squeaked.

'God, are you four or fourteen?' said Peri.

'Cadi's invited me to an audition for *Thousand
Ships*! She says I might get a part in the chorus.'

'What?'

'*Thousand Ships*,' gabbled Nicola. 'That's the
play her brother's producing for the Rep. They're
holding auditions at the CWA hall. They want girls
for the chorus.'

'What's that got to do with Cadence?' asked
Peri. 'Isn't playing the lead in the *Rap Opera*
enough for the greedy thing?'

'Cadi's not greedy,' objected Nicola. 'Merrick's
afraid there won't be anyone to play Psyche. She's
a sort of dancing girl, she's the younger self of
Helen Troy — that's the heroine, you know — and
she's haunting her.'

'Sounds complicated,' said Mrs Christian. 'I'd hate to have my younger self hanging about to haunt me.'

'May I go?' asked Nicola.

'I don't know, Nicky — aren't you already flat out with rehearsals for this *Rap Opera*?'

'I'm only understudy prompt. I don't have to go to every single rehearsal.'

'Surely Cadence does though — isn't she playing the lead?'

'Yes — but —'

'Okay, but I don't want you taking on too much during the holidays,' said Mrs Christian. 'It wouldn't hurt *you* to go Peri. It'll get you out of the house and you're perfectly able to sing.'

'I'm going swimming,' said Peri hastily. She gathered her gear and, shaking off offers from Debbie and Duncan to accompany her, gathered up Skates and headed off for the beach. Only of course she didn't stay there, but turned off to walk back through the rainforest.

It was the first time Peri had been back to her private place since her encounter with Linnet Valeria, and she wondered if the place would be spoiled for her.

Much to her relief, she found the pool as peaceful and welcoming as ever, but after an hour or so she began to wish she had someone other than Skates to talk to. Someone who would answer her but who wouldn't rabbit on or make dumb remarks. Someone like Linnet Valeria, perhaps.

Linnet might be the same age as Dunc and dull Debbie, but it seemed she still hadn't gone over to the enemy. And she didn't like Cadence either, which was another plus. Peri glanced hopefully at the entrance to the grove, but of course Linnet Valeria did not appear. Why should she? Peri had made it pretty plain she didn't want intruders and besides, Linnet had only come in the first place to take pictures for her cruddy calendar competition.

Peri leaned back and daydreamed. Her dad and Carolyn said she had to find a job in the next two months, or else go back to school. There was no use applying for anything this week; no one was hiring or firing over Christmas and New Year. Besides — didn't they know you sometimes had to wait weeks to be called for an interview and weeks more to know whether you'd got the job? Of course they knew. It was all part of their plan to get her back to school.

The trouble was, Peri didn't know what she wanted to do instead of school. It had to be something she'd enjoy otherwise, apart from the money, she'd be better off at Surfside High.

She ticked off the opportunities around Longbeach. Most of the available jobs were concerned with farming and fishing, the hospitality or the tourist industries. She might pick up some work at Coco's or Guiseppe's, but everyone and her dog was lining up to be waitresses for the summer and probably Dad and old Carolyn wouldn't consider waitressing a proper job. Besides — Peri was honest enough to admit that if a customer bugged her she'd probably end up dumping a drink over his or her head and get the sack.

Linnet Valeria was a photographer — that might be fun, but you needed to have a decent camera and they didn't come cheap. Apparently Cadence's brother, Jason Merrick, was doing a theatre course, but he was based in Sydney and the chances of her dad and old Carolyn letting Peri go down there were just about zilch. Music; she'd never taken it seriously, and it involved a heap of training. Besides, only the very talented and the very lucky got anywhere with that. She could always teach it, like Duncan — God — that meant going back to school!

Peri loved the idea of fashion design, but that meant further training. School, again. Hairdressing — she might have gone for that, only her stepmother had been a hairdresser and that was enough to put her off. Maybe she could pick apples or grapes or help cart hay — seasonal work, again. Damn.

Thoroughly depressed, Peri packed up her things and went home, only to find she'd made a big mistake. She'd assumed the audition for the wrinklies' play was going to be that afternoon but she should have known better. Nobody ever did anything on Boxing Day except sleep off their hangovers from Christmas Day. The audition was the next evening, and though Peri did her best to get out of it, Mrs Christian was determined to make her go.

'Nonsense,' she said when Peri protested. 'If you don't go you'll only be slouching around all night, sulking or playing loud music. Go on. You might learn something. And leave Skates behind. They don't like dogs in the CWA hall.'

Peri scowled. They might be able to make her go, but they couldn't make her enjoy it. She took three new fashion magazines and her nail set. If nothing else she could paint nail polish onto the backs of the CWA chairs.

Much to her disgust, Peri had to travel to the audition in the same car as Cadence Merrick and the bug-eyed alien. Cadence's brother was driving. All Peri could see of him from her place in the back seat was a lot of spiky dark hair, broad shoulders and a twinkling earring. He seemed bigger and older since she'd seen him last.

She hunched sulkily over towards the door because Cadence and Nicola were already crammed in the back seat. Naturally, Duncan sat in the front with his old mate — dull Debbie had decided to stay home and run through her part for the *Messiah*. Peri bet her stepmother didn't tell *her* to stop playing her loud music.

'What've you been doing since you got back, Merrick?' asked Duncan in the front seat.

'Oh — this and that. Went to see Tory and old Park. They never change, do they, except Tory's pregnant now. I'm having dinner with them tomorrow — want to come?'

'Isn't Linnet going with you?'

Merick's head jerked irritably. 'Too busy. She *says*.'

There was a little pause, then Duncan cleared his throat and changed the subject. 'What's *Thousand Ships* actually about, Merrick? I don't think I know it.'

'Be bloody grateful you don't,' said Merrick. He had a deep voice, much deeper than Duncan's, and Peri glanced up in surprise. She found her eyes meeting his in the rear-vision mirror and to her disgust, he gave her a wink. The piece of face she could see reflected was not handsome, but looked fearsomely aware and intelligent. God — how could he be Cadence's brother?

'What's wrong with it?' chirped Nicola.

'What *isn't*? God, if only they'd waited for me to get back to them instead of going ahead and choosing a musical themselves!'

'I would have expected them to choose Gilbert and Sullivan, or Rodgers and Hammerstein,' said Duncan. 'That's what local rep groups usually go for.'

'I wish they had, but they picked *Thousand Ships* and now I've got to make something of it. It's the most awful mish-mash you've ever seen — Helen of Troy in modern dress. Helen Troy's an ageing society woman, Menelaus is her wealthy husband who neglects her, Paris is his rival in the corporate stakes. Castor and Pollux are transvestites — and so on — oh, and there's an odd, very fey, very sexy character called Psyche but we need a young dancer for that, not a scone-fed farmer's wife. It's all totally inappropriate for Longbeach Rep. And from what I hear we're going to be horribly short of dancers. The Rainforest Revivalists have poached them all for *their* musical. They're doing *Gaia* and, I can tell you, I'd rather be directing them. I suppose there *might* be some talent in the summer people but I'm not holding my breath.'

Duncan laughed. 'Has it occurred to you that *we* could be classed as summer people now?'

'*No*!' Merrick sounded truly revolted.

'True,' said Duncan. 'You and I, Debbie and Linnet — all the old gang. We only come back in the summer time. And as for the talent — why not con Linnet into dancing? That is, if you're still on speaking terms?'

'Off and on,' said Merrick moodily. 'Mostly off, to tell the truth. She's supposed to be coming tonight, but don't hold your breath.' He paused and added, 'She's pretty friendly with some bloody journo she works with. He's followed her up here! Anyway, she won't dance, because she's already doing the photography for *Ships*. I think the silly fools thought it was family entertainment when they picked the play.'

'Isn't it?' asked Duncan.

Merrick lifted one hand off the wheel and Peri noticed he wore a small gold ring on his little finger. It flashed as he ticked off points on his fingers. 'Rape, incest, adultery, lies, cheating and revenge. What do you think?'

There was a pause. 'Doesn't sound like Longbeach Rep,' said Duncan.

'It ain't.'

Hearing Merrick whingeing on about a job he'd presumably applied for, and accepted — and which was probably going to pay him — Peri was disgusted. What a creep! If Linnet Valeria was trading him in for a new model it showed pretty good judgement on Linnet's part. But what else could you expect from Cadence Merrick's brother? He might look okay, but he was obviously a Cadi-copy inside.

In the hall even Peri could see the audition was a shambles. Apart from herself, Cadence and Nicola, there were only two other young women, one of them pregnant and the other very plump. The rest were old hands who had belonged to Longbeach Rep for years.

'Very fey, very sexy, I *don't* think!' Peri hissed to Nicola as they entered. 'These look like the cast of *The Night of the Living Dead!*'

Nicola giggled nervously, then went with Cadence to sit near the front of the hall. Peri stayed right at the back, where she could see everything but not be seen. This was going to be some night out!

Jason Merrick looked like a falcon in a chook run. He had made no attempt to look like a sophisticated director — he was wearing an old sweatshirt with a rude message across the front — but his three years living in Sydney had had their effect and, like Duncan and Debbie, he no longer looked like a native of Longbeach. Peri couldn't quite put her finger on the change, but it had been obvious in Linnet too — a sort of bemused expression as they looked at the locals as if they were wondering what in the hell they were doing there. As Peri watched, Merrick shook himself visibly and sighed.

'Okay — we'd better get down to it,' he said resignedly. 'You'll all be aware that *Thousand Ships* is a parody of modern corporate warfare. The key character is Helen who is largely passive, but who causes all the trouble. The Menelaus and Paris characters need to balance Helen in the eternal triangle, so I propose to cast these three first, and fill in the other characters afterwards. Who do we have who wants to try out for Helen?'

One of the chooks examined her list. 'We

thought Paula was a natural for that part so why not
try out the men first, Mr Merrick?'

Paula Kerrigan! God! She was forty if she was a
day! Peri saw Merrick frown with disapproval. And
why not? They'd hired *him* to take charge so why
didn't they get in and do what he said?

'All the same I'd like to see everyone in the order
I suggested,' he said. 'Who else wants to read for
Helen?'

There was a non-committal murmur, so Paula
Kerrigan smiled and said she'd start the ball rolling,
but that he'd have to bear with her as she wasn't
much good at sight-reading.

She was right about that, but the two who
followed Paula were even worse, so Merrick
resignedly pencilled her in for the major part. Peri
could practically hear his sigh. She could certainly
see it.

The character of Paris was apparently more
difficult to cast, as there were three inaudible men
who had obviously been coerced into auditioning.
One of the other men was looking at his watch, and
after a while he caught Merrick's eye.

'Can't stay much longer, mate — I've got to get
back to my wife.'

Merrick looked up distractedly. 'Which part do
you want to read for?'

'Menelaus.'

'Then run through a speech for us now.'

The man started reading aloud from the script. It might just as well have been a grocery list. Peri sighed loudly, and took out some chewing gum. This was going to be a long, boring evening.

Peri was wondering if she dared sneak out and go home, when there was a disturbance at the doorway. The man reading for Menelaus stopped in mid-sentence and everyone, including Peri, turned to stare as Linnet Valeria came in, followed by a tall, muscled hunk in a blue sweatshirt and tight jeans. Linnet was wearing a battered old green jacket and tights, which she managed to make seem like high fashion.

'Don't mind us,' she said, but Merrick was tugging at his earring and glaring at her.

'So, you actually made it!' he said, and looked at his watch. 'And I suppose we should be grateful you're only forty-five minutes late!'

'That's forty-six, lover,' said Linnet lightly, but her green eyes looked wary.

'Now you *are* here, perhaps you'd care to introduce your friend to everyone else,' said Merrick.

Peri had been beginning to feel rather sorry for Merrick, seeing the quality of the cast he would be having to work with, but now her sympathy was swinging towards Linnet. So she was late. So what? That didn't give him the right to humiliate her in public! And why shouldn't Linnet have a male friend if she wanted one?

'This is Karl Larssen, everyone,' said Linnet. She was still smiling, but Peri could see a flush of embarrassment, or downright annoyance, on her cheekbones. 'Karl might *look* like an iron man, but actually he's a journalist freelancing for *Arts Unlimited* and various other papers. He's doing a series of pieces about the entrants in the eisteddfod.'

Merrick scrubbed his hands through his spiky hair and managed a weak grin for Larssen. 'Tonight is only the audition, you understand,' he said. 'You'd better come back in a week or so when we get rehearsals underway.'

Larssen flapped a hand. 'No, no, thanks. I'll just hang in here and watch — soak up some atmosphere if that's okay? I've already got some notes on the Surfside High entry — just basic stuff, but I'll have to go back to them again, too.' He looked directly at Cadence and Nicola. 'Didn't I see you two at the rehearsal there?'

Nicola was chewing her fingernails, but Cadence flushed and smiled and nodded yes.

'Cadence Merrick, right?' said Larssen. 'Thought so. I never forget a face.'

Not if it's all pretty-pretty, anyway, thought Peri savagely.

'But — aren't you playing the lead in the *Rap Opera*, Cadence?'

Cadence blushed again and said modestly that she was.

'Then what are you doing here? Spying out the opposition?'

'Something like that,' said Cadence, and smiled.

God, Peri thought, the girl was flirting with Larssen!

While Cadence talked with the journalist, Linnet and Merrick were arguing in hissing whispers. Peri's sympathies began to waver again, and by the time the audition got back on line, she didn't know whose side she was on — but what did it matter anyway? Linnet Valeria had been fun to talk to for a short time, but they would never be friends. As for Merrick — how he could stand to see his sickening sister sucking up to his girlfriend's follower?

Peri lost the thread there, because Merrick turned abruptly away from Linnet and called for anyone who wanted to try out for the part of Psyche. Another fiasco. The first two hopefuls were no good at all. Merrick stared at the pregnant woman in disbelief.

'Oh, the bub will be born before the show goes on,' she explained cheerfully.

'Yes, but there is a scene where Psyche dances and sings,' he said patiently. 'Wouldn't you find rehearsing that a bit difficult?'

'I suppose that lets me out then,' said the pregnant one with a grin.

Nicola wasn't a chance either, for although she was obviously doing her best, her impromptu dance consisted of little more than self-conscious posing to the music put on by Linnet Valeria. As for the singing — Peri cringed in embarrassment and glowered at Duncan. Duncan knew Nicola couldn't sing — why hadn't he told her she shouldn't audition for Psyche?

Merrick's hand went up to tug at his earring again. That was why he probably wore it, thought Peri, to give him something to play with when he was bored out of his skull. That was one reason she had her ears pierced. Then Duncan was leaning over, tapping Merrick on the shoulder, and, unmistakably, pointing at her.

Merrick turned to consider her just as if she was a side of beef. 'Peri? Would you like to try out as Psyche?'

'No thanks,' said Peri.

Merrick stared at her for a few seconds. He had very bright eyes, and a surprisingly sensitive mouth. Peri stared back and, at last, he made a gesture of irritation and turned away from her. 'Well, if that's the way you want it. Is there anyone else for Psyche?' He sounded almost plaintive.

Then Cadence was up, giving her skinned-back hair a quick smooth and her top a tug. 'I'd like to try out, Jason,' she said.

Merrick gave her an exasperated look. 'But you're — oh, hang it. You might as well. Read this speech and then run through the song and dance.'

Cadence put lots of expression into it, letting her voice rise and fall and fluttering her free hand about. Then she handed the script to Nicola and began to dance, and then she sang. Peri had to admit it; Cadence might be a cow, but she was a talented cow — if you liked screechy soprano voices and showy steps. Nicola was looking worshipful, and there was definite approval in Larssen's face. Even the other women who had auditioned for the role were nodding as if they thought the result a foregone conclusion. Merrick, however said something in an undertone to Linnet, who grinned and shook her head vehemently. Merrick threw up his hands and turned away from her.

'I'll have to think this one over,' he said.

It was the plump woman who had auditioned who spoke first.

'Jason, am I right in thinking this Psyche character is supposed to be Helen's younger self?'

'That's one interpretation,' said Merrick cautiously.

'Then I think you'd better cast Cadence. She's obviously the best one for the part and in the circumstances nobody could possibly call it nepotism.' She looked at the others and said good-naturedly, 'If it won't be too difficult directing your sister?'

'You may be sure I'll treat Cadence every bit as badly as I'll treat the rest of you,' said Merrick, and

Peri thought he really meant it. 'Now — for Helen's society ladies — Nicola here will be one extra, and so will you and Liza, but we'll need at least five more.' He glanced up at Peri as he said that, but she carefully studied her fingernails.

Finally, the whole dire performance came to an end. Peri had been yawning her head off for the past hour. There had been a horrible fascination in seeing people, including the bug-eyed alien, make fools of themselves. The only pity of it was that Cadence the cow hadn't made a fool of herself.

Once more Peri found herself mashed in the back seat of Merrick's car with Cadence and Nicola.

Merrick turned to Linnet. 'Want to come with us?'

Linnet shook her head a little too quickly. 'No thanks Merrick. I'm taking Karl round to the caravan park — he's staying there while he does these pieces. See you, all!' She sketched a little salute, then turned and took Larssen's arm.

Merrick shrugged. 'Just as well — if she'd come, someone would have had to sit on the bonnet.' He looked at his sister, 'By the way, Cadence — what do you mean by putting the hard word on me?'

'Who? Me?' Cadence sounded light-hearted — but wary, too.

'You know what I mean,' said Merrick shortly. 'You popped up and auditioned there — the others were so useless I didn't have much choice — ow — what have I said, Dunc?'

Peri grinned savagely. She knew what he'd said, and it didn't need Duncan's low-voiced mutter to explain it to Nicola, either.

'Gee, I'm sorry, Nicky,' said Merrick after a moment. 'I guess I'm just — er — cheesed off.'

'That's okay,' said Nicola, but Peri could hear the hurt in her voice. So, she thought sourly, could everyone else. Did the bug-eyed alien have to be so bloody transparent? But it seemed even bug-eyed aliens had their limits. Nicola turned to Cadence, and said quite sharply, 'Cadi — what's Ms Borrojavic going to say?'

On ya, alien! thought Peri, but Cadence just laughed uneasily. 'I hadn't thought of that. But I don't suppose it'll matter much to her.'

'Not matter that you've gone and landed a big part in a rival musical?' said Peri. 'Go and get a brain, Cadence — she'll do her bloody nut — and I don't blame her! What was it she said about total commitment?' She paused to let that soak in then lifted her voice in a savage imitation of Cadence's tones; '"You can rely on my cooperation in this, Ms Borrojavic." That's what you said, wasn't it? And, "you must be willing to give it every gram of your attention and commitment." That's what she said. And you agreed.'

'I can do both,' said Cadence.

'When Ms Borrojavic finds out, she'll make you into pâté.'

'So, who's going to tell her?' Cadence said sweetly.

'Maybe me,' said Peri slowly.

'You wouldn't be so mean!' Nicola said, of course.

Peri didn't know if she'd be that mean either — but she had no objection to seeing Cadence squirm.

In the end, Peri didn't need to tell Ms Borrojavic Cadence Merrick was moonlighting with the opposition. The local newspaper did it for her.

'Just listen to this!' breathed Nicola on New Year's Eve. She shook out the paper and read the article aloud.

'"Cadence has acting all rapped up.

"Surfside High student, Cadence Merrick, is all set to make a splash at the Longbeach eisteddfod. Clever Cadence has landed not one, but two plum roles in opposing musical productions. The attractive sixteen-year-old, sister of Jason Merrick who is directing one of the two musicals, seems unfazed by the amount of work ahead. 'No, it doesn't bother me that I've got two parts to learn,' says confident Cadence, 'The parts are so unlike one another there's no possible way I could mix them up.'

"Cadence will be playing a leather-clad rapper queen called Rapture Red in Surfside High's *Rap Opera*, and a Trojan dancing girl called Psyche in the Longbeach Rep's production of *Thousand Ships*."'

'Yeuch — stop before I throw up!' said Peri. 'I thought that Larssen guy was writing for an arty-farty arts mag? Looks like *he's* moonlighting now!'

'But Peri,' Nicola said, 'can't you see what this means? Cadi's famous!'

'Yeah,' said Peri. 'She's also right in the shit with Ms Borrojavic. And if you ask me, it'll take more than a pretty smile to have her come out smelling like roses *this* time!'

CHAPTER 10

Peri would have loved to have been a fly on the wall for the next *Rap Opera* rehearsal, but she couldn't think of any excuse for attending. Nicola had made sure everyone knew what sort of mess Larssen's article had dropped Cadence in, and even Peri didn't really want the entire Christian household accusing her of going along to gloat.

Instead, she took herself off to her private place. Or, that's what she intended to do, but she hadn't got more than halfway through the rainforest when she heard a mob of people barging along behind her. She didn't want anyone gatecrashing her pool, so she turned and headed back the way she had come, holding herself aloof and pretending she hadn't heard them. Unfortunately, that was a mistake.

The mob were all boys, about seventeen or eighteen and, Peri realised quickly, a bit drunk. They were jostling and shoving, trying to push one

another into the prickly vines. And if one of them
had ever had a dose of stinging tree, thought Peri,
they wouldn't be so stupid. More fool them! If they
went barging about in a place they didn't know,
they ought to find out about the hazards before the
hazards found them.

Peri had no sympathy for the fools at all — but
she did rather wish she'd brought Skates along for
moral support.

Peri stood aside to let the boys pass her, and that
was a mistake, too.

'Hey babe!' said one of them. He was a good-
looking guy with dreadlocks and shades, which he
slowly removed. 'Heeey! Want to give us a good
time?'

'Rack off,' said Peri.

'C'mon — don't be cold — you look like a hot
little number to me. Right, Spam?'

'Yeah, right,' said one of the others, a big boy
with red hair.

'I said — rack off,' said Peri. She began to edge
past, but the red-head stuck his foot across her path
so that she tripped. She thought she'd fall into the
undergrowth, but the boy with dreadlocks grabbed
her, and held her close against him.

'Ooppsy daisy!' he said. 'Give us a kiss!'

If someone at school had done that, Peri would
have shrugged it off with a joke, or kneed him
where it hurt, or even, if she happened to be in the

mood, done as he asked, but this was different.

'Aw, don't be like that!' said Dreadlocks as she stiffened.

Peri pulled away, but by now they'd surrounded her. Keeping her face stony, she looked around the ring, hoping one of them might show some sympathy. Not all the faces were bad ones — the other two or three looked okay — but there was a look in all of their eyes that scared her badly. It was mob hunger — the thing that turned quite ordinary people into brutes. And not only boys — Peri had seen girls affected the same way, giggling and breathing hard and staring big-eyed at things that ought to have made them feel sick.

Peri tossed around possible solutions. She could try to run, she could scream. She could try to reason with them. She could try to bluff them. Or she could fight back. Damn. She should have learnt some of Ms Borrojavic's judo in Drama. Maybe she could get one of them onside — butter him up a bit. But that idea revolted her. Why the bloody hell *should* she crawl to a load of creeps, just because she was a girl and at their mercy?

'Shove off,' she said, making a huge effort to sound bored. 'If one of you lot had a brain, you'd be dangerous.'

'Yeah?' The pupils in Spam's eyes were huge, and he reached out and gave her a push. Peri stumbled back against a blonde boy who pressed her back against himself for a moment before giving her another push. Not hard — just enough to make her stumble against one of the others.

Peri was terrified, but she was damned if she was going to show it. She looked along the track, but of course no-one was coming, and they were too far away for anyone at the beach to hear if she screamed. There was one thing though. The stinging tree.

Peri took a step forward, and then another, and managed to work the whole horrible ring of them a few metres down the track. The next time one of them pushed her she added to the impetus of the shove herself, cannoning into the blonde boy with the full weight of her body. Her jeans-clad, sweatshirted body. The boy was wearing only ragged shorts and thongs, real he-man stuff, so his bare back came right up against one of the juicy stinging trees. He let out a yelp of pain, batting at himself as if he'd run into a swarm of bees.

'What's up, Cornie? What'd the little bitch do to you?' asked Dreadlocks.

'Just what I'll do to you, if you don't watch out,' said Peri.

The moment's distraction had given her the chance she needed. She dug in her bag and pulled out the bottle of spray-on dye, shaking it vigorously to get their attention.

'The next one to lay a hand on me gets a spray of this!' she said firmly.

'Hey — the bitch has got some of that mace stuff.'

'That's illegal!' said one of them ridiculously. 'You can't have that!'

'And hassling me isn't illegal I suppose!' said Peri. 'Now bugger off!' She flipped up the cap and put her finger on the nozzle. 'This stain lasts a week or more,' she warned. 'It won't wash off, either. I figure I can hit at least three or four of you — now who's it gonna be? You, Spam? Or — what's your name — Cornie?' She swung the can from side to side as if she was hosing off a window.

'It's empty!' said one of the boys.

'I wouldn't bloody bet on it!' said Peri. She tapped the nozzle and a small spurt of dye shot out. 'The next time I do that it's gonna be aimed at your faces. Now piss off!' Peri forced herself to go on glaring at them. One sign of weakness and they'd be on her like a pack of dogs.

One of the boys wavered. 'Hey — that stuff can blind you,' he said nervously.

'Nah — it's harmless, but she ain't worth the hassle,' said another. 'You'd probably catch something off her anyway. She's probably put out more than once, haven't you sweetheart?' He made a kissing noise, and Peri jammed her finger down on the nozzle.

The gush of foaming dye startled her almost as much as it did her assailants, but she leapt past them and ran for her life towards the beach. 'Help!' she screamed. She kept on yelling but when she reached the beach, scratched, sweating and heaving for breath, she was alone. There were a few kids out swimming, but the tide was right out so they'd hardly have heard her.

Shaking, Peri headed for home. Debbie and Duncan were there, endlessly chewing over the *Messiah* problem. Peri ducked behind them and went straight to the bathroom, where she looked at herself in the mirror. Her face looked back at her, sullen as usual, her curly hair was snarled and dotted with bits of grass and twigs. She looked as if she'd been doing precisely what those boys had intended, and with an exclamation of distaste, she peeled off her sweaty clothes and stepped into the shower. Her sweatshirt had drops of green on it, which meant she'd either have to get rid of it or brazen it out with old Carolyn. She could pretend she'd knocked the nozzle when she was digging about in her bag — or she could say she'd squirted it at someone for fun. One thing she wasn't going to do was admit she'd had to use it — she'd given her stepmother too much flack when she'd been forced to carry it about. And now she'd have to get another one.

But after today she had to admit old Carolyn had actually been right. For once.

CHAPTER

11
eleven

Peri was too shaken from the ambush in the rainforest to gloat over Cadence's misfortune, but she heard all about it anyway. Nicola came back from the *Rap Opera* rehearsal overflowing with sympathy and ran on and on about it until even Mrs Christian had had enough.

'Nicky, I'm sure your friend Cadi is upset at being ticked off in front of the whole cast, but she must have known she was running a risk when she took on this other part. And if you consider the two musicals are coming up against one another before the judges, it's not surprising your teacher is annoyed.'

'I'd be ropeable,' said Duncan. 'There's no way the silly kid can give her best to two roles at the same time, and if one of them suffers it's just as likely to be the Surfside effort. I'm surprised at Merrick for encouraging her.'

'If anyone can play two parts, Cadi can,' said Nicola loyally. 'She's always got a lot on her plate, hasn't she, Peri? She likes it that way.'

Peri shrugged.

'Doesn't she?' Nicola persisted. 'She's on the student council at school, and she's sports captain and prefect and she helped organise that recycling drive we had last term.'

Peri, who had been involved in none of these things and hoped she never would be, shrugged again but, eventually, she was forced to admit that if anyone could carry off acting Rapture Red *and* Psyche, it would be Cadence Merrick.

'And none of the cast was actually told *not* to audition for other parts,' said Nicola.

'I expect your Ms Borrojavic thought that was self-evident,' said Mrs Christian. 'It's as bad as playing on opposing teams of a sports match at the same time! So, what's happening to Cadi? Is she having to drop out of one of the plays?'

'No — Ms Borrojavic says she can play Rapture Red as long as she never misses a single rehearsal. And if she slacks off at all, the understudy — that's Cass Tranton — gets it.'

'I can't see why Merrick took her to the *Thousand Ships* audition at all, if that's the case,' said Duncan.

'He thought she might be one of the chorus — and they only have to learn a few songs and make up the numbers.'

'Couldn't he have cast someone else in this Psyche part?' asked Mrs Christian.

There was a pause.

'No,' said Duncan, 'I don't see how he could have. It's not as if there's much time to play with — the eisteddfod's on in five weeks' time. And that's where your *Rap Opera* will have it all over Merrick's thing. School kids are more disciplined about learning their lines and they'll come to peak performance quicker. Unlike us oldies, eh Debbie. We've still got some of that *Messiah* to learn, haven't we? Though it's hardly worth *my* while bothering until I hear something.'

'I've already said I don't mind dropping out,' said Debbie anxiously.

Peri felt ill. Why should Debbie give up her part just to avoid hurting Duncan's feelings? He was meant to be a grown up, after all.

After a while, Peri retreated to her bedroom and rubbed Skates' ears and listened to her Walkman until a cheery horn toot under the window informed her that Duncan and Debbie had gone out. She stayed in her room for three more songs, then went out to the living room where Nicola and old Carolyn were sitting on the couch discussing *Thousand Ships*.

'Give it a rest,' Peri said.

'I think it's interesting,' said Nicola.

'You would.'

'Peri?'

Peri turned to her stepmother. 'What?'

But old Carolyn wasn't going to tell her off about rudeness again, instead, she had put on a sickly smile. 'Your dad and I have been wondering if you'd like to do some sort of summer course, since you didn't want to go in the play with Nicky.'

The woman never gave up! 'I've told you,' said Peri stonily. 'I've had enough of education. I want to get a paying job!'

'Not that sort of course, Peri. Maybe some sort of hobby, we thought. Wouldn't you like to learn ceramics or dancing or tennis? Or even cooking, like Jo? You need to get out more, meet more people.'

'I need a job,' said Peri between her teeth. 'Then maybe I'd have some money to get out *on*.'

'We'd be happy to pay for you, if you found anything you could be interested in,' Mrs Christian added.

But not happy to give her the money itself to blow on clothes or fabric. Peri's Christmas money had amounted to precisely one garment, a skirt which she still had to alter to her own specifications. Peri narrowed her eyes. Her stepmother had walked right into this one. 'Yeah, there is something.'

'Yes?'

'I'd like to take up skydiving,' she said deliberately. 'When do I start?'

ld mean stepping down from her high horse, also seeing Cadence Merrick queening it in red yl, and the less she saw of that cow, the better.

o Cadence was not allowed to miss a rehearsal? t even one teensy one?

Peri's eyes glittered as a brilliant thought hit her. e could put Cadence Merrick out of the *Rap era* if she chose. It would be simple — all she d to do was ring Cadence and pretend to be cola — and Nicola's breathy, squeaky little voice s a cinch to imitate! She could ask Cadi to meet r somewhere urgently, and then ...

Invention began to peter out at that point. The vious thing would be to ambush Cadence and ck her in somewhere. Keep her mewed up long hough to make sure she missed the rehearsal, but e logistics were impossible. How could she find a lace where Cadence's yells wouldn't be heard? In ummer, Longbeach was brimming over with locals nd summer visitors — every loo sported a queue, o did changing rooms. The school would be mpty, but Peri didn't have the keys to Surfside High. And she'd have to let Cadence out eventually, Peri realised, and then there'd be the devil to pay.

'Nah,' she said to Skates, 'she isn't worth the trouble, is she? Not worth the trouble of doing it and not worth the trouble I'd get into for doing it.'

The paper had interviews with four of the other musical entries, too, but Peri only read the one

96

'Skydiving!'

'*Anything*, you said,' Peri reminded her.

'Anything within reason, I meant, and you know it,' Mrs Christian said.

'This is within reason.'

'Peri — skydiving is expensive and extremely dangerous.'

'Excellent. When can I start?'

'Don't be ridiculous, Peri!' said Mrs Christian crisply. 'Of course you can't go skydiving. That's in no way comparable to acting in a musical, and you know it!'

Peri hooked her thumbs in her pockets. 'So you were talking through your hat, as usual,' she said, and walked away leaving her stepmother without a word to say.

Back in the bedroom, Peri arranged herself on the bed and put her hands behind her head. She'd known old Carolyn would renege on a skydiving course. Just as well really, because Peri couldn't stand heights. She wondered what she'd have done if, by some miracle, her stepmother had called her bluff.

Lying there, Peri suddenly flashed back to the episode in the rainforest and shivered. She hoped she wouldn't dream about the ambush and the mob: Dreadlocks, Spam and co.

Peri slept soundly that night, but during the next few days she found that the ambush had shaken her badly. She no longer felt like going to her private place, just in case those same boys were waiting for her. She might not get off so lightly next time. Even if she took Skates with her she wouldn't feel really safe in the rainforest — he might scare a few people but he was as soft as porridge inside. But it wasn't only her special place where she felt nervous — now she hardly felt safe going anywhere by herself.

Once when she walked to Bojangles to eye off their new summer gear she saw Spam swigging a thick shake outside Coco's. She ducked into the hardware shop and hung around, examining a bin of marked-down tools for ages until he'd left the table and headed off down the street. Even then she'd lingered, but then she had happened to see Linnet Valeria walking down the footpath with the journalist — what was his name? Larssen? — so she fell in behind them and dogged their footsteps until she was safely away from the middle of town.

They seemed *very* friendly with one another, and Linnet had her arm around Larssen's waist, but maybe that was only Linnet's way. Peri wondered if the calendar photographs had been developed yet — they must have been, since the closing date for the competition had passed. It would be interesting to see the photographs, but she couldn't go up and ask Linnet in the street, so she turned and hurried home. Though why *she* should have to dodge and hide was beyond her. Surely it was the ambushers

who ought to feel guilty about ru
since they were the ones who'd done

Duncan and Debbie were out, a
had gone to some meeting or othe
Peri had the house to herself. She
newspaper her dad had left lying on
spread herself out on the couch.

'Peace and quiet,' she told Ska
snuffled in agreement.

She turned to the social pages, l
looked boring and old, so she flipped
arts. There was a piece about the *Rap*
interview with Ms Borrojavic and a
picture of the cast, all dressed in amazi
leathers and skin-tight leggings.

With surprise Peri felt a twinge of
could have been one of those amazing fig
hadn't been so pig-headed. She could ha
out with the costumes, even if she didn
act. Designing those futuristic clothes w
been wild, but if she'd been in charge s
have made them less alike — surely pec
post-apocalyptic society wouldn't have bee
mass-produce garments like those.

'The feathers are a good touch, though,'
Skates. 'Wonder if they've been p
someone's chooks?'

For a second she was tempted to go along
Borrojavic and ask did she want any extras, b

about *Thousand Ships*. There was a photograph of the director standing next to a tall and gangly man with glasses and a mild, intelligent face.

"*'Longbeach Rep's* Thousand Ships *director, Jason Merrick, discusses the play with set-designer, Parker Southey ...*'"

'Never heard of him,' said Peri, and turned to the employment pages. The list was pitifully short, especially for jobs around Longbeach. She'd already put her name down with the CES, but they hadn't contacted her for a job interview yet. Peri ran her eye down the column but all the jobs seemed to call for experience, or for own transport, or else they sounded like slave labour. There was no way she was baby-sitting snotty kids for the rest of her life — she'd rather go back to school.

It was boring being stuck around the house all the time, but every time she went out she saw — or thought she saw — one of the ambushers. Once it was certainly two of them, for they were waiting when they saw her coming out of Coco's with Skates. One of them was Spam, the other Dreadlocks, and they turned in unison to stare as she stepped out of the coffee shop. Spam made a kissing sound.

'Get stuffed,' said Peri automatically.

That was a mistake, for it made them look at her properly. Before, they had presumably seen her as just another girl, but now recognition dawned in their eyes.

'Hey, babe!' said Dreadlocks, 'wanna give us another good time?'

Spam caught on quickly. 'Yeah,' he said, closing his eyes in pretended ecstasy. 'Remember the time we had before — weeooo!'

'Trouble, Skates!' Peri snapped, and Skates burst into an obliging volley of barks.

Dreadlocks jumped, then took three or four threatening steps forward. Skates yelped and retreated to safety behind her legs, so Peri hurried away, but she could hear them catcalling and laughing behind her.

She knew she shouldn't feel ashamed, but the meeting had unnerved her and Skates was no protection. So Peri mostly stayed at home after that.

Apart from writing applications for several unexciting jobs, there didn't seem a lot to do. Everyone else in the household was busy — Duncan and Debbie catching up with old friends, her stepmother with her meetings, her dad with his house-painting business and Nicola, of course, acting as Cadence's disciple and attending rehearsals of the two musicals.

Peri was the only one with nothing special to do, and she supposed that was why she finally gave up and went along to a rehearsal of *Thousand Ships* with Nicola. She thought it might be amusing to see how the unpromising cast was shaping up, she might see Linnet Valeria and jog her mind about the photographs — and it would be better than moping around the house all day, or going out with Skates and spending the whole time on the lookout for Spam and Dreadlocks.

And to think Peri had been bothered a month ago because she never had any peace! Now she had nothing *but* peace — except when her stepmother hassled her about doing something. Besides — the rehearsals had moved from the cruddy CWA rooms to the Town Hall, so she could sit up the back in comfort and style.

With this in mind she cornered Nicola and told her she was coming along to watch that night's rehearsal. Surprisingly, Nicola wasn't keen on the idea.

'Merrick mightn't like it,' Nicola said. 'He's cross enough that we've got to rehearse tonight; Ms Borrojavic had already booked the hall for this afternoon, and the Rainforest Revivalists had it this morning. If you turn up it might make him really cranky.'

But Peri said the Town Hall was a public place, wasn't it? and got in Duncan's car next to Nicola. Short of pulling her out, there wasn't very much Nicola could do.

'Just don't say I didn't warn you!' said Nicola. 'He's not going to be very pleased with you — or with me for bringing you. Why don't you go down to Guiseppe's?'

'Because I hate pizza and I want to see the rehearsal. And why should I care whether Merrick's pleased or not? He's only bloody Cadence's brother!'

Merrick *wasn't* pleased, but since Duncan had already dropped them off and gone on to collect Debbie from some friend's place, he said Peri could sit in as long as she kept her mouth shut and stayed out of the way.

'By the way — have you seen Cadence?' he said to Nicola.

Nicola shook her head nervously. 'N-not since five o'clock. Ms Borrojavic kept the leads back for some blocking. I expect she's gone to get something to eat.'

'Damn. I told her to get a lift with Linnet. Go and get yourself ready then — we're late.'

'I'm going to sit up the back — okay?' said Peri.

'Yeah — right — just don't get in the way.' Merrick turned away as if she were of no account, which made Peri feel like doing something to prove otherwise. That wouldn't be too clever, though, so instead, she settled down to watch the rehearsal.

Merrick seemed tense and edgy. Looking at the material he had to work with, Peri didn't blame him, but she did wonder why he kept looking at his watch. Surely Cadence wasn't *that* important to the show? She beckoned imperiously to Nicola, whom she could see peering anxiously towards the door of the hall.

'What's biting little Hitler?' she asked. 'And where's Linnet Valeria? I want to see her about something.'

'What do you want to see her for?' Nicola asked.

'Nothing to do with you. Is she coming?'

'She should be, but she's not here yet. Neither's Cadence,' whispered Nicola.

'Weird,' said Peri in her normal voice. 'Not like Cadi-wadi to miss a chance of strutting her stuff.'

'Shh!' hissed Nicola, bug-eyes swivelling towards Merrick. 'Look, I've got to go. You will be quiet, won't you?'

Peri said no, she was just about to get up and dance the can-can.

'Peri,' Nicola said anxiously.

'Yeah, yeah,' said Peri wearily. 'I'll behave — and is that meant to be a fishtail braid?'

'Why?'

'It looks terrible. If you *must* muck about with your hair, why don't you let me fix it for you again? It looked good last time.'

Nicola stared at her, more bug-eyed than ever.

'Oh, run away,' said Peri. Hoping something would start to happen soon, she settled in a comfortable seat and crossed her legs.

The cast members looked totally boring, and the chorus girls looked dull. She recognised a few of them as rejects from Ms Borrojavic's *Rap Opera* and wondered if Merrick knew. Then she turned her attention to the director. At the audition, she had wavered between feeling sorry for him and annoyed with him, but watching him standing in front of the stage, hands in pockets, exuding tension and impatience, she realised he was really rather attractive, if you liked mean and moody people. The piratical gold earring caught glints of light from the lights and Merrick's expression when he again looked at his watch was definitely dangerous.

Watch out, Cadence! thought Peri with relish. Or — was it Linnet he was waiting for?

Merrick glanced at his watch again then visibly came to a decision. 'All right everyone! We'll skip the prologue and go straight into scene one instead. I shall have a few words with Psyche when she deigns to turn up!'

So it *was* Cadence bugging him. Peri supposed it *was* embarrassing that the only cast and crew members missing were his own sister and girlfriend. Probably they were together, taking photographs for some other competition. Probably all that mouthing-off Linnet had done about Cadence had been hogwash. Peri pushed the thought away, unwrapped some chewing gum and slid it slyly into her mouth, waiting for the next act in the drama. Merrick looked as if he might explode any minute but, as she watched, he suddenly turned business-like.

'Helen Troy and her friends are discovered in her sitting room,' he announced, and suddenly the stage came alive as Nicola and the other women and girls flocked around the woman playing Helen. 'There will be a couch for Helen here — just where the yellow chalk mark is. You'll lounge elegantly on it, Paula, and the rest of you will be sitting on the floor ... Yes?'

One of the older women had cleared her throat discreetly and Merrick was looking at her with ill-concealed impatience.

'On the floor? Surely we're not meant to be bohemians? And what are the white and purple chalk marks for? Surely there won't be two pieces of furniture in the same place?'

'*White* chalk marks?' Merrick looked mystified. 'I don't know anything about *white* chalk marks. Park Southey and I used yellow.'

'Excuse me?' Incredibly, it was the bug-eyed alien speaking up. 'Merrick? I mean, Mr Merrick? The white chalk marks are for the *Rap Opera*. Ms Borrojavic put them there this afternoon. I don't know about the purple.'

Merrick sighed loudly. 'Thank you, Nicola. We shall ignore the white chalk marks, and the purple, and any other colour chalk marks that will no doubt miraculously appear during the next few days. God! This is madness! As for sitting on the floor, the object is to point up the big advantages conferred on Helen Troy by her looks. I want someone to hold a wine glass, someone else to support a mirror.' He pointed to specific people. '*You* can be brushing Helen's hair and *you* can be fetching a magazine.'

Nicola, not among those chosen for bits of business, was kneeling obediently on the floor. She'd get splinters in her knees if she didn't watch out.

'Rhubarb, rhubarb,' said Merrick. Nicola and the other kids looked at him blankly and Peri sighed for their ignorance. Even *she* knew what that meant. 'Say "rhubarb rhubarb",' said Merrick impatiently. 'It gives the impression of conversation. Aquilla, enter and announce Menelaus — run! Pace! Pace!' He looked thoroughly, but thoroughly, pissed off.

The action on stage snailed forward with so many breaks and jerks that Peri gave up trying to make sense of the plot and went back to her study of the director. He was much younger than most of the cast, yet they all seemed to do as he said. Not just Nicola and the other school kids, but the adults too. They deferred to his judgement, even the bossy ones twice his age, and Peri wondered why. In her experience this wasn't the way things happened. At school you did what the teachers said, or got a detention. She'd proved that over and over during her last term. At home, you did what parents said, or got grounded or had your pocket money docked. She'd proved *that* a time or two, too.

But all the time you were growing up no-one ever seemed interested in your opinions or your skills. They *said* they were, they *said* they wanted you to develop self-reliance and initiative, but once you stepped out of line — their line — they pushed you back down where you belonged. Just because you were a teenager and they were adult.

Once you left school potential employers weren't interested either. Not even interested enough to reply to your applications. The CES weren't interested in your opinions, only in why you weren't planning to finish school. So when did the big change take place? How and when had Jason Merrick, only a few years older than herself, got himself into this position of power? Luck? Talent? Or sheer force of personality?

Peri watched Merick closely, and nothing seemed to add up. But he *was* attractive. Mentally, she contrasted him with the guys she knew at school. Some of them were okay, but most had lumpy Adam's apples, bony wrists and spotty foreheads. Or else they were surfie types who pretended not to have any brains. Not that Merrick's looks mattered a scrap to Peri. Since her encounter with Dreadlocks, Spam, Cornie and co, she was off guys, period.

CHAPTER 12

Peri hadn't finished her observation of Merrick when he made an error that lowered her opinion of him considerably.

On stage, Paris had courted Helen who had agreed to an elopement but who insisted on taking her chattels with her. Paris was fed up and Helen went into her seduction routine.

'*Don't you want little Psyche?*' she cooed.

Ugh! thought Peri, and evidently Paris agreed with her.

'*Are you nuts?*' he asked.

'*Psyche! Psyche!*' called Helen. Sounding for all the world as if she was calling a dog!

'Break!' Merrick held up his hands and looked about, obviously hoping to see Cadence. And, of course, she hadn't shown up. 'Okay,' he said, 'one of you girls can stand in for Psyche.' Amazingly, he seemed to be beckoning to Nicola, who was down in the front row of chairs with the other extras. 'Nicola Christian? Okay, Nicola can you come up and go through the motions as Psyche?'

Peri craned her neck and shifted her gum to the other cheek. The man must have rocks in his head. Couldn't he see the bug-eyed alien was scared stiff? But Nicola was scrambling out of her seat with pathetic eagerness. You wouldn't catch me jumping like that at the master's voice, thought Peri.

'How should I come on?' Nicola was asking.

Merrick looked at her sardonically. 'This is just a suggestion, but you might consider using the stairs.'

Peri rolled her eyes. Nicola had really asked for that one. But she'd made it up the steps to the stage and was waiting in sheep-like fashion to be pushed into position. Merrick was still organising Paris and Helen when a door banged down in the body of the theatre. He looked around irritably and Peri realised that Cadence had finally arrived.

Nicola was taking in the situation and retreating down the centre steps and Cadence was dumping her bag and hurrying up the other set of steps to the left — all movement, but no fireworks, yet.

Peri yawned, and reached down to her bag for more gum. Consequently, she missed the next piece of action, but a startled cry from those on the stage alerted her in time to see Cadence tumbling down the steps to land in a huddle at the bottom.

Everyone, except Peri, leapt up and dashed to the foot of the steps; Merrick swore loudly and vaulted off the stage, the plump woman pushed through the mob like a duck through chickens saying loudly that they weren't to touch her, that she had her St John's, that they must be careful or they'd do the girl a mischief. As far as Peri could see, Cadence had already been done a mischief. It seemed all wrong to see Cadence lying there with her pink vinyl bag tangled up in her legs. Peri felt a nervous, unpleasant twinge in her stomach, as if she had somehow ill-wished the girl. She'd wanted Cadence to get her comeuppance, but not like *this* — God, was her neck broken? She was lying in a horribly twisted way and there was blood in her blonde hair.

Peri went on sitting there like part of an audience, while all the others milled around Cadence. Merrick was giving Menelaus the keys to the front office, Peri thought he looked sicker than Cadence. He was holding a pad to control the bleeding until the ambulance arrived. It was the look on his face that got to Peri. He might be bad-tempered and flippant, but he really cared about his sister — anyone could see that.

Nicola sorted herself out of the crowd and came over to Peri. 'D'you reckon we ought to go home?' she asked uncertainly.

'We can't until Duncan comes back for us,'

Peri pointed out to her. 'Not unless you want your mother yapping on at us for not waiting for him.'

Nicola shivered. 'What if she's dead? It'd be my fault. If I hadn't been on those other steps she wouldn't have tried to go up the side ones.'

'That's right, blame yourself,' said Peri. 'If she'd got here when she was supposed to it wouldn't have happened either. It had nothing to do with which flight of steps you used.'

Or with Peri's ill-wishing either.

'It wasn't her fault she was late,' said Nicola. 'She had to stay on at the *Rap Opera* rehearsal and she had to have *something* to eat!'

Peri grunted. Excuses, excuses. Everyone had them. Cadence should have bought a sandwich at the deli next door, or gone without, or not have taken two parts in the first place. Then she wouldn't have been in such a rush and she wouldn't be bleeding on the Town Hall floor. Perhaps this time Cadence Merrick wasn't going to come up smelling like roses. But Peri couldn't be pleased about that. It would have been quite satisfactory if Cadence had slipped and fallen on her bum or split those tight shorts or peed herself or something, but nobody deserved a fall like that one. No-one deserved to land in a huddled heap and bleed all over the floor.

The ambulance came and Cadence was loaded on a stretcher and carried out. A confusion in the doorway sorted itself into the arrival of Linnet Valeria and her friend the journalist.

'What the hell's going on here? Who's hurt?' asked Linnet.

Merrick turned on her and snapped, 'More to the point, where the hell have you been?'

'Look, I've been working,' said Linnet. 'We sort of ran overtime.'

'Oh yes?'

'Look here, Merrick — this is not the only photo job I've got at Longbeach and some I'm actually paid well to do!'

'Cadi's had an accident. And if you'd given her a lift the way you were supposed to, it wouldn't have happened.'

'Hang on just a bloody minute!' said Linnet, grabbing at his elbow. 'I went to your place but she wasn't there.'

'Get out of my way,' said Merrick in a low angry voice. 'I'm going with the ambulance. If you want to be useful, you can sort this lot out and lock up.'

He walked out, leaving Linnet Valeria standing in the middle of the doorway with a bunch of keys dangling from her fingers. She watched him out of sight then held out her hands appealingly. 'What's this all about? I called round for her but she'd already left — what did the kid do to herself?'

Someone began some low-voiced explanations but Linnet continued to expostulate. Larssen came over to Peri. 'The girl who's hurt — it's Cadence Merrick — right? The *Rap Opera* girl? The director's sister?'

Peri was about to answer when Linnet interrupted. 'I suppose you're after a bit of a sob-story for your precious magazine! You're not to print any of this — understand?'

'I'm concerned about the girl, that's all,' said Larssen, injured. 'She's a bright kid, and seems to have everything going for her.'

Linnet threw up her hands. 'Forget it. Go home. I give up.' She turned to the remaining cast members. 'Let's get cracking. Helen and Paris — you ready?'

Peri whistled under her breath. Surely this mad woman wasn't going on with the rehearsal! How could she, with a major character hurt and the director away at the hospital? But it seemed that Linnet did mean to carry on. She put aside her camera equipment and burrowed through the pile of papers beside the director's chair. 'Here's the master plan,' she said, 'so let's get on with it. Where had you got to in the script?'

When Linnet spoke out everyone looked blank, so Peri stood up. 'Helen just called out for Psyche,' she said.

Linnet acknowledged her with a quick, unrecognising nod. 'Good. Then we'll need — let's see — Helen and Paris and a stand-in for Psyche.' Her green-eyed gaze swept through the cast. Nicola half-raised her hand, and Peri felt she could read her half-sister's mind. She'd already been chosen by the director, so why not? But Linnet's gaze passed her by. Flushing, Nicola lowered her hand.

So there, thought Peri, but her heart wasn't in it. She felt a sudden distaste for the whole business. 'The show must go on' and all that — but what if Cadence did die? Linnet Valeria had gall and a half to press on as if nothing had happened. And all those spare women — Nicola included — hovering like vultures waiting on Linnet's decision. They must think they were getting a second chance at a major role.

Then the tension broke as the woman playing Helen Troy spoke up from the stage. 'But Linnet, of course you must stand-in for Psyche. After all, you know the play, and we've always thought you should have had a part.'

Linnet gave her a sudden slanting grin. 'And I've always told you I wouldn't stand for Merrick directing me.'

'Merrick isn't here,' said Paris.

'For God's sake,' said Menelaus, 'can we please get on? I've got to get home.'

Paris nudged Helen and she spoke the cue again: '*Psyche! Psyche!*'

Linnet turned and ran lightly up the steps, to kneel at Helen Troy's feet. '*Psyche is here. Why am I called again?*'

For a while, Peri found herself really admiring Linnet Valeria. The woman played Psyche, amplified and relayed the director's instructions from his master plan, and even found time to take the occasional photograph of the cast. Peri had thought Merrick was in control, but he had *nothing* on Linnet. She was magic, but after a while, admiration gave way to a prickle of discontent. Linnet seemed to be increasingly leaving aside the plan and following her own whims. *Thousand Ships*, thought Peri sourly, looked like turning into 'The Linnet Valeria Show', with Psyche out-acting everyone else. At least Cadence wouldn't have done *that*. Oh, she'd have tried, but she wouldn't have had the talent. And the sycophantic idiots of the cast were lapping it up — she'd thought it only Merrick who could control them like that. Now it looked as if they'd follow anyone, just like a load of sheep.

'She's great, isn't she?' Nicola said adoringly, when the rehearsal finally ended. It looked as if Linnet Valeria was going to take over from Cadence as top of Nicola's particular hit parade.

Peri shrugged perversely. 'How d'you make that out?'

'The way she carried on for Merrick — she's saved him having to do this blocking rehearsal all over again.'

'That wasn't what he wanted her to do, though,' said Peri. 'I think she's an interfering bitch.' She'd decided she was definitely on Merrick's side, in this.

'But — if she hadn't taken over, the whole thing would have flopped,' said Nicola.

'She should have just locked up like he said. It could have been done properly next weekend.'

'But next weekend Menelaus's son is getting married.'

Peri snorted.

'Merrick will be grateful to have it all done for him, anyway,' said Nicola.

Peri looked at her with contempt. 'You're just so stupid. You know that? Really stupid.'

Surprisingly, Nicola turned on her. 'So how would *you* know what Merrick wants? You don't know him. You haven't even been to a rehearsal before today!'

'I know if I was a director I wouldn't want someone else taking over!' said Peri.

'She knows him better than either of us,' said Nicola. 'She's his girlfriend, after all.'

'So what?'

'So if you're going to marry someone you get to trust their judgement!' said Nicola in a high voice. 'And Linnet's every bit as smart as he is, anyway!'

Peri snorted. 'You're just so naive — and if she's going to marry Merrick, what's she doing going about with that git, Larssen?'

'That doesn't mean anything, Cadi says. Merrick and Linnet have been an item since Year Ten.'

Off and on, Merrick had said. Mostly off, at the moment.

'And Cadi's judgement is so damned good she's practically killed herself — much you seem to care about that. She's supposed to be your best buddy, remember?' Peri replied.

A horn tooted, making them both jump. 'Hurry up, girls!' said Duncan.

In the car, Nicola chattered on about the awful accident and how great Linnet Valeria had been. Debbie made the right noises, Duncan asked concerned questions and Peri slumped in the back seat and scowled.

When they got home, there was more carry-on about the accident. Mrs Christian wanted to know exactly how it had happened, Mr Christian wanted to know if Longbeach Rep had insurance. They all went on and on.

'What happens to the show now?' asked Debbie. 'Will Cadence be all right, or will Merrick re-cast the Psyche part?'

'Oh, Linnet's playing it now,' said Nicola. 'She was wonderful — directing, taking pictures, and playing Psyche at the same time.'

'Sounds like Linnet, all right,' said Debbie drily, and Peri blinked. Somehow, she'd thought Debbie was a member of the Linnet Valeria Fan Club, too.

'If Merrick doesn't watch it, she'll have him out of a job,' agreed Duncan.

They seemed to find it amusing, but Peri
wondered if they meant it underneath. Perhaps
Linnet *was* trying to take over her boyfriend's job.
It was nothing to do with her, of course, but she
was starting to see that Linnet Valeria was the same
sort as Cadence — trying to run everything. And
look where that had got Cadence! Right out of two
plum roles and into hospital — or the morgue. She
shivered. What if Cadence *did* die? Would Linnet
Valeria just keep on keeping on?

cHapteR

13

The news came next day, via Nicola, that Cadence had broken a bone in her back.

'God!' said Peri. 'Does that mean she's crippled for life?' She wouldn't have wished that on Cadence, even if she *was* a little cow.

'Apparently not,' said Nicola cautiously. 'She's going to be in hospital for a while though — and she probably won't be able to go back to school at the start of Year Eleven. Linnet says she's all wrapped up in a horrible big plaster, like a tortoise's shell.'

'Oh, *Linnet* says!' mocked Peri. 'I suppose she pissed off there right away, just to make sure the poor little cow really *is* out of the show.'

Nicola looked stunned. 'Peri, you're a real airhead! If Linnet had wanted to play Psyche she would have said so, right at the beginning. You were there when Merrick asked her to do it. You saw her say no.'

So she had, but Peri couldn't resist trying to wind up the bug-eyed alien. 'I bet she plotted it right from the start,' she said evilly. 'Probably greased the steps, even.'

'*Peri*! She couldn't have!'

'No, she couldn't have,' said Peri, abruptly bored. She yawned. 'That's that for Cadence then — are you going to visit her? Take her some grapes and sympathy?'

'When she's feeling a bit better I shall,' said Nicola with dignity. 'Why don't you come, too?'

'I just might at that,' said Peri, and left Nicola staring. 'By the way,' she added over her shoulder, 'can I come and see one of the *Rap Opera* rehearsals sometime?'

Nicola gaped at her, then shut her mouth abruptly. 'I guess so. What for, though?'

'What do *you* reckon? I want to see if anyone else manages to break their neck.'

Nicola wasn't the only one surprised at Peri's sudden interest in the *Rap Opera*.

'Peri Christian!' said Ms Borrojavic. 'I thought you wanted nothing to do with any holiday activities?'

'I thought I could watch,' Peri said. 'It's not a crime, is it?'

'Obviously not,' said Ms Borrojavic. She waved a hand down in the body of the hall, where a handful of kids from school and some of the summer people had come to gawk. Peri glanced at the costumed rappers already on the stage. Cass Tranton looked amazing; spiky red hair bristling with plumes, her tight costume clinging like a second skin.

'It's astonishing the interest we've had since we began dress rehearsals,' said Ms Borrojavic in a dry voice.

Peri found herself casting her gaze around the hall at the summer people. None of them looked familiar and she breathed a sigh of relief. Ridiculous to feel hemmed in by the thought of running into the ambushers again — a bunch of idiots. She wondered if she'd managed to hit any of them with the spray-on dye. Spam and Dreadlocks hadn't been green — maybe she'd hit Cornie and the others though. They seemed to have left Longbeach. Then she wondered what they would have done to her if she hadn't managed to get away. '*Give us a bit of fun,*' they'd said, but she'd bet it wouldn't have been fun for her.

Ms Borrojavic was calling the rehearsal to order, ignoring all the gawkers. 'Chorus — I want the *Rapture* routine first — hit it!'

There was a short pause, then the chorus flocked onto the stage.

'Rapture Red's the one to lead,
Rapture Red — she holds the creed,
Rapture Red's the best we've seen,
Rapture Red's our rappin' queen!
Rapture!!!!!'

'Jump Rapture — now,' urged Ms Borrojavic. 'Lead colours — Blue and Green — flick your hands out towards Rapture. On the beat, Yellow and Fawn do the same. Teal and Silver — no, no, no! Again! Cass, go off and come back on, and see if you can make that jump a bit more vigorous. Take off on the first syllable — *Rap*-ture! Right?'

Somewhere during proceedings, Linnet Valeria arrived with Larssen, and the real rehearsal was suspended while Linnet set up supposedly live action shots in colour and black and white. Peri stared at her moodily. Did the woman have her finger stuck in *every* pie?

As Peri had first thought, Cass Tranton was making a good job of the lead. Cass's plain, sharp features were probably much better for the role than Cadence's pretty-pretty face. So why hadn't Cass been cast as Rapture Red in the first place? Because the Cadences of this world always got in first, that's why. Unless they fell down the stairs. And what happened to them then? Did they still manage to come out on top, even lying in hospital in a horrible plaster cast? Was Cadence even now organising everyone on Kids' Ward — or had they put her in Women's Surgical? — or had she finally dropped her bundle?

Having not much else to do, Peri decided she'd go along to the hospital with Nicola and find out. And of course, she *wasn't* going to gloat, and she certainly *wasn't* interested in the current state of affairs between Jason Merrick and his girlfriend, Linnet Valeria.

Not much she wasn't!

The fact was Peri had painted herself into a corner, and it hurt. She'd always known she wasn't popular, but she'd seen that as the price she paid for her prime goal of pleasing herself before any others. If pleasing someone else was what she felt like doing, she did please them. Otherwise, she didn't. It was a direct and simple philosophy, and she had always been quite satisfied with it. Pleasing someone for the sake of it — that stank, especially since most people seemed to live to get under her skin. She felt no obligation to please her family. She hadn't asked to be born, and she was only *really* related to her dad and the bug-eyed alien. She also did little to please the other students at Surfside High. They had to take her or leave her. Consequently, many of them left her. Why couldn't they be more like Skates, who loved her warts and all?

As for guys — Peri'd never really fancied one before. She'd thought the ambush in the rainforest had put her off the whole tribe, but now she'd discovered it hadn't. Not really.

She'd had a few crushes on pop stars in her time, although she'd kept them ruthlessly private. So she was experienced enough to recognise the symptoms when a new one struck, though — and like it not, one had struck her now. And the object, naturally, was Jason Merrick, who was not only Cadence's brother, but an adult at that. She should have guessed what was going on the very instant she'd started wavering in her allegiance to Linnet Valeria. After all, was it likely that Peri Christian, who reckoned most guys were the pits, would take the side of one of them against a bright, go-getting woman?

It was *not* likely, therefore there was more to it than met the eye. Linnet definitely had what it took to get what she wanted. Presumably, Merrick had it too, but he didn't make it obvious the way Linnet did — or was this opinion just another symptom of her crush?

She could hide her head in the sand and suffer or she could fight it off. *Or,* she could follow through and see what happened. And why not? He'd said he was 'mostly off' with Linnet at the moment and if, on the odd chance, he *did* happen to be available, why shouldn't he be interested in Peri? No reason — but if he was, he'd certainly shown no sign of it yet. And she wasn't one to chase a guy who wasn't interested, so she'd better put him right out of her mind while there was still time. So far it was only a little crush — she was sure she could overcome it if she tried.

CHAPTER 14

Cadence Merrick looked utterly shocked when Peri and Nicola walked into the ward. She *was* in Women's Surgical, with a broken leg on one side and a skull fracture on the other, and she looked scruffy and very uncomfortable in her unwieldy plaster cast.

'How are you feeling, Cadi?' asked Nicola.

Bad move, thought Peri, sitting down in one of the chairs and crossing her legs. How do you reckon the poor cow's feeling? And Cadence did seem down — the famous Barbie doll hair was half-shaved at the front and what was left was lank and greasy.

'Oh — it's not so bad,' she said, but she looked as if she might cry.

'You look awful!' said Nicola.

Bad move number two. Cadence's hand went defensively to her hair. 'I'm going to have it all cut short tomorrow,' she said. 'Sort of spiky, like Cass's, you know?'

Like Cass Tranton? Did Cadence know Cass had taken over the Rapture Red part? Apparently she did, because she brought up the subject herself.

'How's Cass going?' Cadence asked.

'She's great!' said Nicola. 'I mean — she's not as good as you were, but she's doing okay.'

'I hope she's more than okay,' said Cadence steadily. 'I hope she's good. It's a wonderful part and I'd hate to see it ruined. Not that I will see it — I'll be stuck in here for ages.'

Cadence looked depressed, and Nicola couldn't contradict her. 'I guess Ms Borrojavic will organise a video of the last dress rehearsal,' she offered. 'You could arrange to see that.'

'Don't be so bloody silly,' said Peri fiercely. 'She doesn't want to see it, do you Cadence? And I don't blame you. I wouldn't want to see it either, if I were in your shoes.'

'Sorry — I was only trying to cheer her up,' muttered Nicola.

'You're not succeeding. Hey Cadi — any cute doctors round here?'

That got a half-smile. 'You've got to be kidding,' said Cadence.

'Looks like I've wasted a visit then,' said Peri. 'Unless that yummy brother of yours is coming in?'

Cadence Merrick and Nicola turned identical open-mouthed stares on Peri, and she felt her face growing warm. She had no idea why she had said that — she thought she'd meant it as a flip jokey comment like other girls made, but it hadn't quite come off. Probably because both Nicola and Cadence knew perfectly well Peri just didn't make *that* sort of flip, jokey comment.

Cadence smiled slightly. 'Sorry to disappoint you, Peri — no, he's not.'

'Darn it!' said Peri, clicking her fingers, and again it rang hollowly.

'Have you had any other visitors today, Cadi?' asked Nicola quickly.

'Only Linnet and Karl Larssen,' said Cadence.

'Thrilling, eh,' said Peri drily.

'It was very nice of them to bother,' corrected Cadence. 'It was nice of you two, too. I'm sure you've both got better things to do. How's *Thousand Ships* going, Nicky? Linnet didn't say much about it — she did show me some photos she took of me though — she said she was going to use them in a calendar girl competition, but she didn't seem to think they'd win. Would you believe she said I'm *too* pretty?' She gave a rather cracked laugh.

'Have you got any of them?' Nicola asked.

'As a matter of fact, I have. They're in that drawer over there — can you reach?'

Nicola opened the drawer and took out a sheaf of photographs. 'Oh — these are excellent!' she said.

Peri thought her voice sounded a bit forced, so she leaned over to look. They were pictures of Cadence posing in a swimsuit, leaning on a rock, jumping over a wave — surfacing, hair streaming — all very bright and sporty and, as anyone could see with half an eye, *much* too pretty-pretty to win any prizes in a serious photographic competition. But that wasn't what was bothering Nicola, she was sure. No, the bug-eyed alien was nearly in tears because the contrast between Cadence-*then* and Cadence-*now* was too cruel.

'They *are* great, aren't they?' Peri said heartily. Too heartily. Cadence might have been a poser, but nobody ever said she was unintelligent.

'They're nice all right,' she said listlessly. 'But it will be a long time before I look like that again — correction; I'll *never* look like that again.'

'Of course you will!' said Nicola, appalled. 'A few weeks in hospital and you'll be as good as new!'

'My hair,' said Cadence. 'I'm having it all cut off, remember? It's just too difficult to manage with this plaster. And it took me five years to grow it this long and in another five years I'll be twenty-one. As old as Jason. And all because of one little slip on a stair.'

It did seem rotten luck, but Peri reminded herself it hadn't started with the slip on the stair. It had started when Cadence had taken on too much. She'd gotten away with it for years, so she'd obviously expected to get away with it this time. Only she hadn't. Or no — perhaps it had really started because Cadence had never believed she could fail. Wherever her fall had its beginnings, it was tough for Cadence, but Peri wasn't wasting too much sympathy on her. Cadence would survive. Her sort always did.

'Hey,' Peri said, 'I reckon short hair might really suit you, if you stopped skinning it back and let it curl around your face a bit.'

CHAPTER

15

Peri went to the next rehearsal of *Thousand Ships* as a sort of dare with herself. If it had been Linnet in charge again, she would probably have walked out, but Merrick was back, putting his actors through their paces with considerable vigour. There was a truly cataclysmic row between him and Linnet over the interpretation of the Psyche part, but Linnet gave in, then danced and sang her way through the part so sweetly it was a shock when the scene finished and she dropped out of character and glowered at Merrick in a fashion that was decidedly un-loverlike.

When Peri found her gaze resting on Merrick all the time instead of only some of it, she realised her dare had miss-fired. A full-blown crush had struck, and she really didn't want it after all. Adoration from afar was okay when the subject *was* a pop star, but it was a damn nuisance when he was locally available. And it really was nonsense to think Merrick'd be interested in her — if he thought of her at all it was as Duncan's kid sister, just like Nicola.

Peri was darned if she was going to act like those silly girls at school did sometimes — hanging about, bumping accidentally-on-purpose into whatever hunks they happened to be pursuing. She wouldn't lower herself to that. So give up, Peri thought, before you make a bloody fool of yourself.

She stayed away from *Thousand Ships* rehearsals after that, but it didn't help. She had bought another can of spray-on dye, and, since she hadn't seen Spam and co for a while, she began to hang round Coco's and Bojangles again. Unfortunately, coming out of hiding meant she seemed to see Merrick everywhere, buying razors or apples or picking up the post, or occasionally heading down to the beach with a surfboard. Once, he was on a motorbike with Linnet sitting behind. Peri was on the point of hailing them and asking Linnet if she could see the photographs, but they passed without seeing her, anonymous in their black helmets and leathers.

Since staying away from the rehearsals was achieving nothing, Peri went back to watching Merrick, sitting invisibly in row H, witnessing the play take shape, and cringing whenever Nicola made one of her little mistakes. Nicola was pathetic. She had a way of looking doubtfully at whoever was closest whenever she had to make a move, obviously asking for reassurance that she was doing the right thing. She'd left off skinning her hair back, but had taken to gelling it instead. Peri often braided or plaited hers, but she had the broad forehead and strong cheekbones to carry it. Nicola looked more like a bug-eyed alien than ever.

Karl Larssen often showed up at the rehearsals, too, but whether he was hoping for another spectacular accident or simply wanted to moon over Linnet Valeria wasn't clear. There didn't seem to be any love lost between him and Merrick. He tried to chat Peri up once or twice, but she turned a cold shoulder and he soon gave up. She wasn't interested in cut-price Schwarzeneggers, but she found she *was* rather interested in the undercurrents that went on while the play took shape.

After a time Peri began to see evidence that she was not the only one who suffered from an unrequited crush. Several of the younger women openly adored Merrick, while the woman playing Helen Troy and the bloke playing Paris were definitely flirting in real-life as well as in the play. And things between Linnet and Merrick seemed to have fallen to an all-time low. Alone among the cast members, Linnet refused to take direction. She made no outright rebellion, but made her displeasure known more subtly by hesitating a few seconds before doing whatever he had asked her to do.

'Tone it down, Psyche, you're over-acting!' Merrick kept saying, but Linnet didn't.

Peri moved forward by degrees until she was sitting quite close to the action. Merrick seemed to accept her presence, and had even taken to exchanging wry glances with her whenever a cast or crew member did something especially idiotic. From this he progressed to the odd greeting or farewell, and then to an occasional request for her to run a message or fetch some coffees.

Peri, who had never been anyone's slave, found herself as foolishly flattered as the silly spaniel down the road who cringed and fawned whenever Skates looked his way. In bed at night she kicked herself for being so weak, but the off-hand grins Merrick gave in exchange seemed more than enough at the time. Peri despised herself heartily.

'God, Skates, I'm just so *stupid*,' she said, hugging her dog one night. 'It's all my own fault, too. I've only got to stay away from him!' But she couldn't do it and though Skates was as loving as ever it no longer seemed enough.

About two weeks after Linnet had taken over the Psyche role, she accosted Peri as she entered the hall. 'Oh — Peri isn't it?'

'Yeah.' Peri raised her eyebrows scornfully. Today she detected a certain glow about Linnet, something which gave her an odd feeling of apprehension. The woman looked as if she'd had a great night — but who had she had it *with*?

'Remember those photos I took of you in the rainforest?' said Linnet without preamble.

Of course she did. She wasn't a moron. 'For the calendar competition,' Peri said.

'Yeah — it was a bloody rush to get it all in on time, but they came up pretty well. I entered the best three shots of you.'

'What about Cadence?'

'What *about* Cadence?'

'I saw some of the ones you took of her ...'

'Oh. Yeah. I entered some, but I knew they weren't suitable.'

'Yes they were,' said Peri perversely. 'I saw them. They were just what you see on postcards and things. The ones of Skates and me weren't like that. I didn't pose or anything.'

'That's just it,' said Linnet. 'You didn't pose. If you knew how rare it is to find a subject that doesn't pose ...'

'Yeah, yeah.' Flattery would get her nowhere. 'So what about it? I mean — you never even bothered to show them to me, so I thought they couldn't be much good.'

Linnet looked mildly offended. 'Of course they were good. What do you think I am? A bloody amateur?'

'S'pose not.'

'S'pose not!' mimicked Linnet. '*S'pose not*! Well, we won.'

'*What?*' Peri stared, appalled. 'I'm not a calendar girl!'

'It's not a title or anything. The thing is, one of my photos of you won a cool two thousand, so here's your cut. I couldn't pay you or promise to pay you before, because it would have voided the rules, so this is just a present with my thanks. And, by the by, you were right about that mutt of yours. He came out a treat.' She handed Peri an envelope and passed on, metamorphosing into the

Psyche character as she mounted the steps to the stage.

After a bit, Peri recovered her wits and opened the envelope. Inside were four, fifty dollar notes. Peri stared at them suspiciously and then put them back and carefully stashed the envelope in a pocket. Two hundred dollars for *not* spitting in Linnet Valeria's eye that day in the rainforest. It almost made up for the fact that she hadn't been back there for weeks. Not since she'd met those creeps.

But thoughts of the money kept intruding. All that for ten minutes' work! Incredible. But still it didn't make sense. What was this competition really about? Where would her picture be shown? And to whom? And what the hell would kids at Surfside say if it came out that she'd been posing for a *calendar*?

By now Peri had grumpily accepted the fact that she'd have to go back to school, unless a miracle occurred and she was offered a job.

Slowly, she moved down to her seat near Merrick. He must have heard the news, because he turned and gave her a cheerful thumbs up and said, 'Good going, Periwinkle: you're the only subject Birdy doesn't bitch about from here to Christmas. Talk about her hating to be directed by me — that's nothing to the way I feel about being photographed by her! Ever thought of going in for it?'

'Photography?' Peri felt her cheeks redden and

hoped the hall was dark enough to disguise it. *God*, what sort of shape was she in? He only had to speak to her and her knees turned into noodles.

'Photographic modelling. According to Birdy you've got the right angles or something — *No* Psyche, hold it right there! You're upstaging Helen again!'

That was the end of the conversation, and Peri wondered if Linnet could have interrupted deliberately. Surely not. The way she messed Merrick around, she couldn't object to his passing the time of day with Peri. And that was all he had been doing. Passing the time of day. She couldn't delude herself it was anything else — but maybe it could be, if she played her cards right!

Peri watched the rehearsal to the end, but she hardly saw a thing. The money crackled in her pocket, and temptation crackled in her mind. The temptation to make a serious play for Jason Merrick after all. She wasn't going to make a fool of herself by being obvious, but there wasn't much time: soon the eisteddfod would be staged and after that, Merrick would presumably go back to Sydney. In that way, he was a pretty poor prospect for a boyfriend, but Peri wasn't after a long-term relationship. She was after an experience and she could think of no-one she'd rather gain it with.

Mr and Mrs Christian were quite bemused by the success of Peri's photograph. It and the runners up in the competition were published in *Arts Weekly*.

'I've never had much use for those too-pretty girls who used to win beauty pageants,' said Mrs Christian rather tartly, 'but now we seem to have one of our own!'

'Peri hasn't won anything, Mum,' pointed out Nicola. 'It was Linnet's picture that won. Peri was only the subject. Linnet took some of Cadi Merrick too, and it could just as easily have been one of those that won.'

'Obviously the judges liked our Peri better.'

'It was Skates they liked,' Nicola joked. 'He's much prettier than Peri.'

'Gee thanks,' said Peri, but she couldn't help being a bit pleased. There was something about the picture — about the way Skates' upraised muzzle led the eye to Peri's own face in the picture — that made the whole composition striking and memorable. She wondered if she could get a copy of it to frame.

'Skates eh!' Mr Christian flicked the article with his finger. 'There's no accounting for tastes!'

There *was* no accounting for taste, was there? Linnet Valeria seemed to have forgotten whose girlfriend she was meant to be. She arrived at rehearsals with the hunky Larssen, and he often picked her up afterwards. Peri had seen them more than once strolling hand in hand through the mall or drinking cappuccinos in Coco's. Once, she even saw them down on the beach. Larssen was smoothing block-out over Linnet's white shoulders, and from the look in her half-closed eyes she was finding it a very pleasant experience.

How could she possibly prefer the muscle-bound Larssen to Merrick, even temporarily?

But it looked as if Larssen's interest in Linnet was anything but temporary. One day when Peri arrived at the hall the pair of them were standing at the back of the seating, discussing something.

'C'mon, Linnet, you know we make a great team,' she heard Larssen say, 'let's go for it!'

'Yeah, yeah! I've told you I'm considering Tory Southey's offer.' Linnet's voice was mocking, but Peri noticed that when Larssen put his arm round her shoulders, she didn't move away.

'Your looks and my talent ...' Larssen said.

'Don't you mean *my* looks and *my* talent?'

A door banged open behind them and Merrick walked into the hall. He nodded to the pair, said good evening to Peri, then turned away towards the stage, whistling through his teeth as if he hadn't a care. Peri stared at him in bewilderment. *Did* he care? If she'd been Merrick, she'd have felt like giving one to Larssen — or Linnet.

Then she noticed Merrick's hands, white-knuckled. He did care, all right.

The rehearsal began, and right from the beginning, there was trouble. Linnet was on stage — she was always a spirited actor — but today she went right over the top.

'Tone it down!' said Merrick angrily, in the interval while everyone else slurped coffee and soft drinks. 'You're detracting from the major characters.'

'Psyche is Helen Troy's alter ego,' argued Linnet. 'She *is* a major character.'

'Absolutely!' snapped Merrick. 'so stop upstaging the original.'

'Psyche is Helen as she still sees herself.'

Merrick glared at her. 'Stop it, Birdy! If you go on as you are we'll have Paula Kerrigan walking out and not even you can play both parts at once.'

'Oh, I don't know,' drawled Linnet. 'I'd have a pretty good go!'

Merrick flung away from her and went to hassle the scene shifters, who had misplaced a chair. The whole exchange had been carried on in angry hisses, inaudible to the rest of the cast, but Peri, in her now-customary seat behind the director, had heard it all.

Linnet made a rude gesture at the departing Merrick then noticed Peri and checked. Her face cleared. It was strange, like seeing a wind-swept pool suddenly calm. 'Peri,' she said, shaking back her hair. 'I've been meaning to have a word with you.'

Peri went cold, but surely Linnet wouldn't be two-faced enough to accuse her of hanging round Merrick. She hadn't been — she'd been watching the rehearsals. 'Yeah?' she said guardedly. 'What about?'

Linnet slid into the seat beside her. 'What do you do with yourself?'

'What d'you mean?'

'Are you still at school?'

Oh-oh — was this the beginning of a *dear-aren't-you-a-little-young-for-him* lecture?

'I've finished Year Ten,' Peri said sulkily, 'and my dad's hassling me to go on to Year Eleven. I can only leave if I get a job, he says. Fat bloody chance of that, since he won't let me work with him.'

'You might be interested in joining Tory's then, at least as a part-timer.'

'Probably not.'

'Look. My friend Victoria has started an agency called "Tory's". Comprehendez vous? She's Parker Southey's wife — him over there.' She pointed to the tall lanky set designer who was now attempting to soothe the still-bristling Merrick.

'What sort of agency?' Peri asked.

'Basically it's a model agency, but that's not all,' said Linnet. 'Tory teaches make-up and hairdressing — she's a beautician — and some business skills. By the time you'd finished her course, you'd know a lot about modelling, and you'd have a good grasp of the basics of business management. She's also looking into a dress design course to complement the others.'

'So?' said Peri.

'So, are you interested?'

'Why would I be interested?'

'Some of the work is photographic modelling,' said Linnet, as if explaining to an idiot. 'I did portfolios for the latest lot of students and — unless those shots of you were a fluke — I'd say you were a natural.'

'Gee thanks.'

'No credit to you,' said Linnet drily. 'You just happen to have the right proportions and colouring. Not to say bones to die for. The camera loves you.' She frowned. 'Whether you have the right attitude is another matter.'

'Model agencies are sausage machines,' said Peri.

Linnet laughed. 'Tory doesn't turn out sausages. No-one will ever look at you and say: "Oh, she's a *Tory's* student", because ...'

Merrick's voice cut in ruthlessly. 'Psyche! Get yourself up here!'

'What's in it for you?' asked Peri quickly.

'Tory's asked me to buy into the agency,' said Linnet. 'So naturally I'd rather have easy subjects to photograph. Think about it. Even if you don't want any work you can't possibly lose by it.'

'How much does it cost?' asked Peri.

'No fee — it works on a percentage,' said Linnet. 'You pay for your portfolio: after that, Tory's takes a proportion of your earnings — if any. Of course —'

'Birdy! Get yourself up here!'

'Heil Hitler!' Linnet got up and strolled towards the stage.

Peri stayed where she was, half-watching the action, half-considering Linnet's proposition. It sounded much too good to be true. But — and there were a couple of hefty buts — her photograph had won a national award for Linnet and, if Linnet was telling the truth, there would be nothing to lose by going along with it. Whether a modelling course would satisfy Mr and Mrs Christian as a feasible alternative to Year Eleven was another matter.

Peri considered every angle, but she still couldn't see what harm it could do to go and see this Tory person. So, when the rehearsal finished, she ignored the hovering Nicola and went up to Linnet and Merrick.

'About this agency of yours,' she said to Linnet, carefully not looking at Merrick. 'How do I get to it?'

Linnet dug a pencil out of her pocket and scribbled a name and phone number on a bit of paper. 'It's in Sunnyside. Here, give Tory a ring and say I said so.'

Peri pocketed the paper and went to join Nicola. Behind her, she heard another low-voiced argument break out.

CHAPTER

18
eighteen

Peri knew there would be a fuss at home if she told them about her plans, so she kept her mouth shut. She telephoned Victoria Southey next day, and was agreeably surprised by the result.

'Peri Christian; you're Linnet's model — right? Park says you watch the rehearsals sometimes. Perhaps you'd like to come in and have a chat with me this afternoon at two. How are you fixed for transport?'

'No worries,' said Peri, which wasn't true, but near enough. If she couldn't con a lift out of anyone or catch a bus, she could ride her bike. Unfortunately, when it came down to it, near enough wasn't good enough, for her bike had two flat tyres and Nicola's was too small. The buses were too late and Mrs Christian had a committee meeting and was unimpressed by Peri's claim that she needed to be in Sunnyside for a job interview.

'First I've heard of it,' she said suspiciously.

'You just don't want me to get a good job!' flashed Peri. Which wasn't very clever, to say the least.

'Settle down, Peri,' said Mrs Christian. 'You know your dad and I want you to have a good job. And the way to get one is to finish your schooling!'

In the end, Peri conned Debbie and Duncan into giving her a lift, by making up a wholly fallacious story about a pregnant friend who needed cheering up. Well — Victoria Southey *was* pregnant, according to Linnet, and probably *did* need cheering up.

'We'll certainly take you,' said Debbie, 'the thing is — it's got to be now — Dunc's got an appointment down the coast at one-thirty.'

With bad grace, Peri agreed. That meant she had to skip the careful preparations she had planned and go just as she was. She was over an hour early, too, so she had Debbie leave her in the mall.

'How are you getting home?' asked Debbie, but Peri said curtly she'd catch the bus. She didn't want dull Debbie muscling in on her affairs.

Sunnyside was a real tourist trap, full of revoltingly-named 'Sunny' places. There was a pharmacy called Sunnyslipslopslap, a joke shop called Funnysunny and a coffee bar called Sunnysideup. Not to speak of Mrs Merrick's Sunnypots.

To kill time, Peri went into Sunnysideup and ordered a sunny-ccino. It looked exactly like any other cappuccino to her, and she was moodily scooping up the froth when the door chimed its revolting little tune and Jason Merrick came in. Peri's stomach seemed to drop away and she concentrated on spooning more sugar into her drink while she wondered what, if anything, she should do. As it happened, she didn't need to do anything, for Merrick approached her.

Casually, she looked up, trying to look as if she hadn't seen him come in. 'Hi Merrick. Sit down if you want to.'

'Thanks Periwinkle.' Merrick slid into a vacant seat. He caught the eye of the waitress and ordered a sunny-ccino for himself and a fresh one for Peri, then stripped off his black motorbike jacket and dumped his helmet on a spare seat. After that, he met her curious gaze with a reassuring grin. 'One's never enough, is it?'

'Depends what you're talking about,' said Peri curtly. She pushed away her empty cup with the giveaway syrup in the bottom and applied herself to the new cup. Then something else registered and she looked up. '"Periwinkle"?'

'Bad habit of mine, renaming people,' said Merrick. 'Birdy's always on my back about it. What's it short for, anyway?'

'Nothing,' said Peri. 'It's from an operetta.'

'*Iolanthe*,' guessed Merrick. '"The Peer and the Peri".'

Of course. He would know that. And she bet even old Carolyn didn't know it. Her mum had named her — named her and run out on her within a few months.

'Could have been worse,' drawled Peri. 'Could have been Iolanthe. What would you have called me then?'

'Io,' said Merrick instantly. 'After the moon. It's volcanic, you know.'

'Io?'

'As it is, you're irrevocably Periwinkle to me. Sorry about that.'

'Who're you then? The Golden Fleece?'

'Jason's such a God-awful name I prefer to style myself Merrickus Secondus — Merrick the Less.'

'God,' said Peri.

'Not quite. Although James the Less may have been His younger brother ...'

Peri shook her head. She had no use for the surreal. 'Where's Linnet?' she asked, getting to the point.

Merrick's face darkened. 'Probably at so-called work. Linnet Valeria and I are no longer close friends — speak of the devil!'

'What?' Peri looked up.

'Don't look, Periwinkle, you'll turn into a pillar of salt. Or I will. Some people,' added Merrick savagely, 'are never satisfied.'

'I don't know what you're talking about,' said Peri.

'Birdy has just come in with Arnie Schwarzabugger — I told you not to look!'

Peri intercepted a frigid stare from Linnet Valeria and an embarrassed one from Karl Larssen and looked away.

'They work together a lot.' She wondered why she was making excuses for Linnet.

'True,' said Merrick. 'But there's also the fact that she refused to have lunch with me. Claimed to be much too busy on a job in Longbeach. I ask you — is this Longbeach? Looks more like Sunnyside to me.'

'Oh.'

'Talk,' said Merrick tensely. He reached out and took Peri's hand. 'Rhubarb, rhubarb, rhubarb.' Smiling in a way that chilled her, he lifted her hand to his lips. Peri snatched it away and pushed back her chair. Crush or no crush she wasn't going to be used like that.

'Rack off!' she hissed.

'Sit down,' said Merrick.

'Why the hell should I?'

'Finish your coffee. I'll be good.'

Peri sat down.

Merrick sipped his own drink. 'Sorry,' he said morosely. 'It was a lousy idea anyway — straight out of a romance novel.' He slapped his left hand with his right. 'Down, boy. Are you coming to see how *Ships* fares in the eisteddfod?'

'I hadn't really thought about it,' said Peri warily.

'Think now,' said Merrick. 'I reckon you've had enough sneak previews. Why not come as my official escort on the Friday night?'

'Why?'

He shrugged. 'Why not? It's a big occasion — performance, judging, party afterwards. Plus Birdy's given me the flick, and Cadi's still on the sick list. Besides — I rather fancy being seen with the Calendar Girl. The other guys can all drool from afar.'

Deputising for Linnet Valeria. And for Cadence. Peri meant to refuse angrily, but when it came down to it she couldn't. 'Okay,' she said. 'Only ...'

'Strictly business. I know the drill.'

Peri swallowed. 'Right.'

'Great,' said Merrick. 'I'll call for you at six-thirty Friday week — and don't wear anything floaty, because I might be on the bike if Ma wants to use the car.'

Peri nodded. The reference to time made her glance at her watch and she leapt up with a yelp of alarm. 'God — I'm late!'

'What for?'

'I've got an appointment with Victoria Southey.'

'That's right. So Linnet said.' Merrick beckoned the waitress and pulled out his wallet.

'Together, sir?'

'No,' said Peri, but Merrick said they were and where was she parked?

Did he think she was old enough for a licence, then? 'I'm walking,' she said flatly.

'I'll take you then, since I made you late.'

It wasn't the first time Peri had been on a motorbike, but she couldn't suppress a squeak of alarm as Merrick wove his way through the post-lunch traffic. Imprisoned inside his spare helmet, she felt cut off from the world, her knuckles ached from clinging on but her fingertips, anchored to Merrick's jacket, burnt. Her knees were shaking by the time Merrick pulled up at the Southey house, and not just from the speed.

'Okay?' Merrick steadied the machine with one foot and lifted his visor. 'How are you getting home?'

'I'll hitch,' said Peri, unbuckling the helmet with unsteady fingers.

'Come off it!'

They were still glaring at one another when the door opened and Parker Southey came out. 'Peri Christian — and right on time. Hi, Merrick, got time for a coffee?'

'Sure,' said Merrick. 'That way I can wait and give Periwinkle a lift home.'

Parker Southey raised an amused eyebrow. 'I take it we can expect Linnet any minute?'

'I bloody hope not! If I never see her again it'll be too soon.'

Parker glanced at Peri and looked away again. 'I'm sorry.'

Merrick also contemplated Peri. 'Don't be,' he said, blowing on imaginary burnt fingers. 'T'were a lucky escape. Birdy's found someone more her own weight to suck dry.'

Vaguely uneasy, Peri followed the men into the house. So Merrick was going to take her home, was he? That could mean he was interested — or simply that he was keeping an eye on the kid sister of his old mate. But there were other things to worry about just now — like the forthcoming interview.

Peri was ushered into an office, where she was received by an obviously pregnant woman who introduced herself as Victoria Southey.

'You mustn't think your fortune's made if you sign up, because it won't be,' she said frankly, after the opening preamble. 'There are no guarantees for either of us in this business. But if you have nothing else on your horizon I think you'd find Tory's worthwhile, if only as an interest. Of course, if you want to finish your schooling first, that's fine. You could still sign on part-time and come in full-time in a year or so.'

'Who else is in it?' asked Peri.

Tory mentioned a few names, none of which were familiar.

'It started pretty casually, when I gave a niece of Park's some tips. She passed on the message to some of her friends and after a while I found I had three or four clients, so I set up officially. I've been working part-time but now —' she patted her smocked front '— it seems the right time to put my trust in my own judgement and see how I go. I've asked Linnet Valeria to join us as our resident photographer — but you don't want all our history at once. I'll get Park to bring in some coffee and meanwhile, you can have a look at some of my students.'

Peri was pretty full of coffee already, but she obediently took the scrapbook of cuttings and began to leaf through.

'Classes run Tuesday through to Fridays, with some Saturdays and evenings,' said Tory when she came back. 'Not everyone comes to every class, of course. There are different aspects which interest different students, and some students have day jobs. These are my moonlighters ... this boy is a trainee accountant. The girl in the lingerie ad here is a nurse. And these two missed out on uni this year, and are marking time.'

'What do I have to do?' cut in Peri.

'I have an agreement for my people to sign. It's quite informal really, just says that you will pay Tory's a twenty percent commission on any work you gain through the agency and, naturally, that you won't accept work elsewhere without clearing it with me first. In return, I try to set up jobs for you — all respectable — and provide an opportunity for you to learn various skills. Why not talk it over with your parents and see what they advise?'

'No way,' said Peri. 'I mean — I'd like to join.'

'I'll give you a contract to have a look at then. Take it away and consider for as long as you like. How old are you by the way?'

'Sixteen,' said Peri.

'I thought you'd be older.'

'Does it matter?'

'Not really, but it does mean you'll need to have an adult countersign the contract.'

'I make my own decisions,' said Peri, frowning.

'Of course,' said Tory, 'But it's a legal requirement. Unless you want to wait until you turn eighteen.'

Peri didn't want that. 'I'll show it to my stepmother,' she said sullenly.

Parker Southey came in, bearing a tray of coffee things. Merrick followed him and put his arms around Tory in a bear-hug. 'Two for the price of one!' he said, patting her front.

'Unhand my woman,' said Parker, but he didn't seem annoyed.

'Merrick and I are *very* old friends,' said Tory, seeing Peri's astonishment. 'Go back a long way, don't we?'

'God, don't remind me.' Merrick turned to Peri. 'Tory used to knock about with my cousin when we were kids. I had the most awesome crush on her when I was fourteen and she was —'

'Watch it, boy-o!' said Tory, waving a finger under his nose.

'Anyway, she met Park and never looked my way again. End of story.'

The conversation turned to *Thousand Ships*, and Peri heard and stored up lots of gossip about the cast. In a way it was fun to hear the inside news, but in another she found herself feeling ever more regretful that she wasn't part of it all. Even Nicola would have a better right to go to the party Park and Tory were apparently going to host after the show — and she'd only missed out because she'd been too pig-headed to try out at the audition.

After a while, Parker glanced at his watch and reminded Tory that she had another appointment booked for three o'clock, so Peri and Merrick took the hint and went out.

'Where to now?' asked Merrick.

Peri tucked her contract into her jacket and zipped it up, eyeing him uncertainly. 'Home, I suppose,' she said. And, rather to her disappointment, that was where he took her.

Peri was put out to find her stepmother parked in the driveway, removing groceries from the car. She frowned as Peri dismounted, but her face cleared as she recognised Merrick. 'Jason! How nice of you to give Peri a lift home. Are you looking for Duncan? He's not here just now — he and Debbie have gone down the coast. Dunc's got an interview for a job.'

Typical, snarled Peri to herself. Duncan's got an interview! And if it had been any other bikie who'd brought Peri home, old Carolyn would have been up in arms. Because it was Jason Merrick, old acquaintance of Saint Duncan, all was beer and skittles.

'You needn't have bothered, though,' went on Mrs Christian. 'If the silly girl had let me know when and where I could easily have picked her up.'

Like hell.

Merrick looked quizzically from Mrs Christian's friendly face to Peri's sulky one. 'No problem,' he said, and took himself off.

'Really, Peri,' said Mrs Christian. 'You shouldn't have imposed on Jason like that. He's very busy with the play and all.'

Peri swallowed a rude retort and helped carry in the groceries. She wanted her stepmother kept sweet until she'd signed the contract.

Mr and Mrs Christian received her news with surprise and some suspicion. 'I don't know, Peri,' said her father dubiously. 'A modelling course? It sounds a bit ambitious on the strength of one lucky break. And what about school?'

'It wasn't my idea!' said Peri defensively. 'I was asked, and that doesn't happen to everyone, believe me!'

'Victoria Southey,' said Mrs Christian, snapping her fingers. 'I know that name — of course! Di Gilligan's girl, over at Sunnyside. She used to do my hair at Sunnystreaks.'

'Now you've sorted out her pedigree,' said Peri coldly, 'maybe you'll sign the contract. It won't cost you a thing. I'll pay for my portfolio with my Calendar Girl money.'

'Don't rush us, Peri,' said Mr Christian. 'This isn't exactly a *job*, now is it? And if you want to study design and stuff like that, why not do it at school?'

'Because this is what I want!' Peri insisted.

'I don't know,' said Mr Christian again. 'You reckon this is on the up and up, Caro?'

'I might ring Di,' mused his wife.

'God!' said Peri. 'Just sign the bloody thing!'

Mrs Christian telephoned her friend Di, and worked the conversation around to Tory's. Next, she telephoned Linnet Valeria. Finally, she spoke to Linnet's mother, who seemed puzzled but who said yes, Linnet was involved with an agency called Tory's over at Sunnyside but no, she couldn't tell Mrs Christian anything about its success rate and wasn't it the Christians' Peri whose photograph had ... wonderful! So she was thinking of going into it seriously?

'Well?' Peri asked her dad, heavy with sarcasm, when Mrs Christian had presented her findings.

'Seems okay to me,' said Mr Christian. 'And the contract's quite straightforward, as these things go. Peri can render it void any time in the first year by simply not attending any classes for three months, or she can arrange to put it on hold for any time up to two years — so long as she does no modelling work for any other party in the meantime.' He exchanged glances with his wife, then took a pen from his top pocket and signed the contract. 'There you are, Peri. And I hope you stick to this longer than you stick to most things!'

'This won't keep you from going back to school as well,' put in Mrs Christian. 'You could attend weekend classes during the term.'

Peri ignored that, and, to forestall more parental cold water, she retreated to the bedroom where Nicola was already asleep. Leaving the door slightly ajar, she was rewarded by a soft murmur of voices.

'I don't know — modelling —'

'Only temporary ...'

'... keep her out of mischief I suppose ...'

'... better than sitting about ...'

'... she'll soon get tired of it ...'

Peri closed the door and slid into bed. So that was what they thought. They could think what they wanted. She turned restlessly onto her back and made plans. She could post the contract tomorrow — or, better still, go straight to Tory's in the morning. That would show them!

Life was looking up. On Saturday it had been flat and boring, enlivened only by her crush on an unattainable Merrick. Now Merrick had finally broken up with Linnet, had stood her a coffee and actually invited her to go to the eisteddfod as his official date. Which probably meant precisely nothing, but who could tell? If she could only keep him away from her stepmother and her father! He had not asked her how old she was and she had the idea he thought she was at least eighteen.

More concretely, she had the uncharted territory of Tory's to explore. Peri sat up and set her alarm clock, untouched since her last day at school, for seven o'clock. She'd looked pretty scruffy for the interview: tomorrow she'd show Tory what she was made of.

'You're not going out like that!' exclaimed Mrs Christian, the next morning.

'Bit of a bum-freezer, isn't it?' said Mr Christian with a grin.

And Nicola just gaped at her like a half-wit.

Peri sat down cautiously. Her skirt was much tighter and shorter than it had been when she had bought it from Bojangles with her Christmas money. She had always been good at sewing but even the split at the back scarcely rendered it fit to be sat in.

'Did you sew yourself into it?' asked Nicola, fascinated. 'How do you go to the loo?'

Peri ignored her.

'Peri?' said Mrs Christian.

Peri sipped coffee. The skirt was quite uncomfortably tight, so she decided to skip toast and just have cereal.

Behind her back, Mr and Mrs Christian exchanged baffled glances, but when Peri said she was catching the early commuter bus to Sunnyside, Mrs Christian just sighed and asked if she'd be in for lunch.

'I'll get something there,' said Peri and got moving before her stepmother could start rabbitting on about sandwiches being cheaper to make than to buy.

The telephone rang, and she lingered on the doorstep, but it was for her stepmother. 'Duncan!' Mrs Christian exclaimed, and then, 'A whole year with the option for two more? That's great —'

Peri scowled. 'I'm off then,' she said, but her father was rattling the newspaper and only Nicola looked up from her breakfast to wish her luck.

Victoria Southey seemed pleased but not unduly surprised to see Peri. 'Make yourself comfortable and I'll introduce you to the others,' she said.

There were six students that morning, two boys and four girls. Peri cast an appraising glance over the boys and discounted them: two of the girls looked self-assured, two were giggling nervously.

'Basic make-up should be seen but not seen,'

said Tory. 'So wipe off any gunk you've got on your faces and see how you go with this lot — oh, and anyone who wants a bit of extra experience can come along on Wednesday week and help with the make-up for Surfside High's entry in the eisteddfod. It's called *Rap Opera*, so you'll have to unlearn all I'm going to teach you now and go for broke with the wild greasepaint.'

The eisteddfod was running for a whole week, with solo and group performances in monologue, music and dance taking up the mornings and afternoons. The musical play section was spread right across the five nights, with one performance each evening. Unlike the other parts of the eisteddfod, the plays were not free entertainment; the organisers had felt that most groups and societies wouldn't want to rehearse a demanding schedule for no income.

The Rainforest Revivalists kicked off the week with a performance of *Gaia*. Nicola went with her parents, and Peri, to her surprise, went with Jason Merrick.

'C'mon, Periwinkle, you're an expert on *Thousand Ships*,' he said. 'You've got to see the opposition.'

The Revivalists did a good enough job, Peri thought, but the music was dweeby and besides, she could hardly concentrate on the action on the stage. She was in her old seat in row H, but the hall was different when crowded with people, and Merrick was sitting beside her. She was wearing the short, tight skirt she had worn to Tory's, and she had a feeling Merrick didn't really approve. Certainly, Linnet Valeria had never worn anything like it.

But he's not going out with Linnet, he's going out with *you*, Peri told herself. She was no Nicola, to turn herself into a carbon copy of anyone else. Nevertheless, she found herself tugging at the skirt uncomfortably, and wished she hadn't worn it. And that really annoyed her because she wasn't used to caring what anyone thought.

On the Tuesday night, they saw *Dance of Death*, performed by a group calling themselves The Sunnysiders. It was an original play written by the members, and they had apparently been determined to live down their name, for it was dark, depressing, badly lit and so long that Peri fell asleep before it finished. She was horribly embarrassed when she woke to find the lights up and the cast, still clad in their rags, skeleton suits and shrouds, bowing. She glanced guiltily at Merrick to see if he had noticed, but he had his eyes on the stage. She began to clap, and Merrick nudged her. 'Hey, don't forget they're the opposition, Periwinkle!'

He put his arm round her shoulders as they left

the hall and she felt herself melt. Something that had never happened with any other guy. She shivered a little.

'Cold, Periwinkle?' asked Merrick, but she was aware he was thinking more about the play he had seen than about her.

Careful, careful! she thought. Don't be stupid, or you'll put him off.

Having seen two of the five plays, Peri began to view *Thousand Ships'* chances in a better light — Merrick's hard work and bullying of the cast had resulted in a much more professional finish to the play and even Linnet Valeria, who seemed to thrive on battles, had apparently stopped winding up her ex-boyfriend to concentrate on giving a smoother performance. And Park Southey's scenery was much more professional than what she had seen up to now.

The *Rap Opera* was a roaring success on the Wednesday night. Peri had reluctantly turned down Merrick's standing invitation of a ride to the hall to go early and help with the make-up with the rest of the gang from Tory's. She was the youngest, but watching the two boys, Nick and Tezza, clowning about with the greasepaint, she felt much older.

Of course, Tory's students didn't get a chance to make-up the leads, but Peri found herself confronted with Aaron Wilkes, a boy she'd known slightly in Year Ten. Aaron was part of the rapper chorus, and he was fairly trembling with stage-fright. Peri told him sharply to keep still while she drew zig-zag lightning streaks on his face, but she really felt quite motherly — after all, he was still a school kid and she'd signed her passport to freedom.

Once the cast was all ready, Peri went out into the hall. Merrick had already come in, and he was talking to Nicola, who was one of the scene-shifters for the *Rap Opera*. Peri felt a spasm of jealousy — but that was nonsense. The bug-eyed alien and Merrick! Ridiculous! Presumably Nicola was picking up the latest news about Cadence. She turned to make her way to the other side of the rapidly-filling hall, but Merrick turned and saw her, grinning and beckoning. 'Hi Periwinkle — finished your treachery for the day?'

'It wasn't treachery, I was undercutting the enemy by spiking their greasepaint,' said Peri. Suddenly, she felt buoyantly cheerful. Merrick had had no need to call her over and she settled in the seat beside him, close enough that their shoulders could brush occasionally, not so close as to seem to be hanging all over him, and waited expectantly for the *Rap Opera* to begin.

Tonight should have been Cadence's big night, but watching Cass Tranton in the role it was difficult to imagine anyone else playing Rapture Red. Peri had seen the *Rap Opera* in rehearsal twice, but now, watching the snap and crackle of Ms Borrojavic's performers, she remembered something Duncan had said to the bug-eyed alien; '*And that's where your* Rap Opera *will have it all over Merrick's thing. School kids are more disciplined about learning their lines and they'll come to peak performance quicker*'.

Even sitting with Merrick, his shoulder warm against hers, she felt an enormous surge of envy. *She* could have been part of this. Maybe she wouldn't have played Rapture Red as effectively as Cass, but she could have easily out-sung the girl who was playing Goldcoast. And her own spiral curls would have looked great on the glittery yellow costume. So why hadn't she auditioned for Ms Borrojavic's thing? Because she hadn't wanted the hassle and the commitment? Because she hadn't wanted to spend the time? No, thought Peri miserably, it wasn't that. The reason she hadn't auditioned was the same as the reason she hadn't auditioned for *Thousand Ships*. Because she couldn't be bothered and because she hadn't wanted anyone else to think she cared about getting a part. And that, for a girl who'd always thought she didn't give a stuff what anyone thought of her, was a hard pill to swallow.

While she was still fighting with the unwelcome discovery she had made, she felt Merrick's breath against her ear. She jerked away.

'Hey, it's okay,' Merrick said. 'I'm not going to bite you — I was just going to say we might as well give up and take our marbles and go home.'

'Huh?'

'*Thousand Ships*, sweetie. We haven't a prayer against the hot rappers of Surfside High. And they even wrote the piece themselves!'

'So, the Sunnysiders wrote their own piece.'

'Yeah,' said Merrick acidly, 'and it showed. This time it didn't, and the judges will have to give them top marks for it. Kids doing a musical by kids for kids — what could be better? Unless of course they'd had the forethought to have a kid direct them ... Whereas the poor old *Ships* cast are all laying way below their true ages — except Nicky and her gang.'

'And Linnet.' Peri couldn't help mentioning it, although the name felt wrong on her tongue.

'Oh — Linnet.' Merrick considered. 'Birdy's the wild card. If she acts to capacity ...'

'We might still win?' said Peri jealously. She wanted *Thousand Ships* to do well, but not if it was all to be due to Linnet.

'God no! We'll lose for sure! The *last* thing Paula and co need is Birdy out-acting them all over the place. Haven't you seen what happens to them? They just go through their paces like they're sleepwalking, watching Birdy turning *Thousand Ships* into the Linnet Valeria Show.'

Peri had thought something similar herself. She was stumped for words.

'She does do it, you know,' said Merrick. 'She just can't help it — has to be the centre of attention.

165

The only hope for *Ships* is that Linnet restrains herself for once.'

'Can't you tell her?' Peri asked.

'Me?' Merrick sounded amazed. 'Me tell Birdy?'

'You're the director, aren't you?' Peri's voice came out louder than she intended, and the people in the row ahead, who had been collecting their belongings and settling down to hear the judges' preliminary report, turned around to stare at her. 'So direct her! It's your job on the line if she mucks up.'

'By God — so it is!' said Merrick. He leaned sideways and dropped a kiss on Peri's head. 'Thanks for reminding me of that small fact, Periwinkle! Now hush up and listen.'

Peri hushed up as ordered. The judges, as expected, gave a glowing preliminary report for the Surfside High team, although they wouldn't be giving the actual scores until the grand presentation on Friday night after *Thousand Ships*, the last of the five musicals, had been performed.

Watching Cass and her rappers, still lit up on a performers' high, Peri again felt a stab of envy. If she had the chance over again ... but if she'd played a big part in the *Rap Opera* she wouldn't be sitting here with Merrick, would she? She tried to take some consolation in that fact, but seeing Cass's glowing face, seeing her vivid gestures as she talked to Ms Borrojavic, she came to the strange conclusion that she would have traded places with Cass, now, tonight.

How she'd feel about it tomorrow, she had no idea, but then — how would Cass would be feeling tomorrow, when the *Rap Opera* was over, and there was nothing to do but wait for the final result?

cHapter 20

The *Thousand Ships* cast was lucky, in a way, for they got to see all the opposition before their own performance. In another, there was the risk of being discouraged or under-rehearsed, for the hall was in use for the five preceding days and they would have to manage with a final run-through on Friday afternoon, back at the CWA rooms.

As Peri was dutifully clapping the announcement of the fourth entry, (*Joseph* from the Reef Bay Musicales), two latecomers entered the hall. They pushed rudely past the ushers, then elbowed their way along the row to sit down not far from Peri and Merrick.

Spam and Dreadlocks. Peri stiffened at the sight of them. They *couldn't* be the same ones who had hassled her after Christmas. They had been summer visitors, and she'd thought them long-gone from Longbeach now. Still it *was* them and their voices, as the ushers tried to remonstrate with them, were horribly familiar.

Peri sank down in her seat and tried to pretend she wasn't there. Not that she was physically afraid of them in such a public place, but what if they started up again as they had outside Coco's? The hall was full of people who knew her, teachers and other Surfside students — not to speak of the *Thousand Ships* cast, most of whom had quite accepted her as Merrick's gofer. Then Spam and Dreadlocks did see her. They nudged one another and Spam deliberately blew her a kiss. 'Hey gorgeous —'

Merrick must have noticed her unease, for she felt him glancing at her several times. 'What is it, Peri?' he asked at last.

'Those guys — over there,' whispered Peri.

Merrick turned to give them the once over. 'Those kids in row G? What about them?'

Kids? She supposed they were, compared with Merrick. But kids could be frightening.

'They — they're staring at me,' she said at last.

'Stare back then,' said Merrick with a grin. 'They're probably envying me my date.' He settled back and put his arm round her shoulders. 'Hey — they're really bothering you!' he said, feeling her sudden tension.

'Yeah — they — they ...' Suddenly, to her bewilderment and disgust, Peri began to cry. The first tears welled out just as the lights dimmed, but

Merrick must have noticed, for he brought his free hand up to touch her face. 'Periwinkle?' He sounded concerned, and Peri, terrified she was going to start howling, muttered excuses and fumbled her way out to the aisle.

Merrick caught up with her as she reached the double doors through which the audience had entered. He stopped her with a hand on her shoulder, and Peri swung round.

'Periwinkle —'

'I'm all right!' she snapped, but a big sob came out in the wake of her words.

'No you're not,' said Merrick, frowning. 'Come out in the fresh air and tell me what's bothering you. It can't just be a few stares — you must be used to that.'

She bit her lip, horribly embarrassed. Why hadn't she simply sat quietly and ignored them? If they'd made a nuisance of themselves they would have been put out of the theatre. Instead, she'd made a sight of herself by rushing out as if *she'd* done something wrong. And maybe she had. Maybe she'd *wanted* to make a big scene and have Merrick chase after her. She just didn't know.

'Look,' she said, 'I was just being stupid, you know? Those two kids — them and some others — gave me a hard time in the rainforest a while ago.'

'What sort of a hard time?' Merrick sounded angry.

'Oh — you know, pushed me around, called me a few names. They didn't really hurt me, but they could've, if I hadn't held them off with a spraycan of dye.'

'Good on you! And you got away okay? Before they — before they did anything more than push you?'

'Yeah.'

'Did you tell your parents?'

'Look,' said Peri, 'I didn't tell *anyone*, okay? I just hoped they'd go away, and I thought they had, but these two seem to have come back.' She swallowed. 'Every time they see me they carry on like they did tonight. Just like it's some big j-joke or something.' Her mouth began to tremble and she sniffed, hard. 'That's all. No harm done. I guess they'll go away once they've finished their holiday.'

'I guess they'll be going away a little sooner than they think,' said Merrick coldly.

'No, Merrick — don't —'

'Don't what? Don't belt them up? Don't be funny. I'm going to take you to the copshop and you're going to tell the cops.'

'No I'm not. They'd only say it wasn't them, or that I'd asked for it, or something.'

'No-one believes that line anymore,' said Merrick, but he didn't sound so certain. 'Maybe it wasn't such a good idea to go walking by yourself though, Periwinkle.'

'And why bloody shouldn't I walk by myself?' hissed Peri.

'You saw what happened when you did.'

'It isn't fair,' she said bitterly. 'Why should women have to go around in mobs like sheep just because bloody men are animals? Oh — sorry. I forgot. You're a man.'

Merrick laughed shortly and patted her cheek. 'You're really something, Periwinkle. But if it makes you feel any better, even guys aren't all that safe walking alone. I've been jumped myself — although all they wanted was money. Rotten world, isn't it?'

'Yeah,' said Peri. She dragged out a tissue and blotted her eyes. 'Has my make-up run?'

'You look like a panda, but then, you always do. Feeling better?'

'Yeah. Yeah, I really am! Let's go in — and if those guys slag me off I'll — I'll scream.'

'That's my girl,' said Merrick. He kissed her upturned face. 'Now, let's get back in, otherwise the show will be over.'

So it would. And of course he wanted to watch it. The eisteddfod was on, and tomorrow was the big day and after that — Peri blinked. After that? She had no idea at all.

As she and Merrick re-entered the hall, there was a sudden yell from the darkness. The lights went on, and two stout uniformed figures appeared from the ticket box to investigate the source of the disturbance. A few minutes and much cursing later, the stout ones were escorting two boys from the hall. Peri was unsurprised to see that they were Spam and Dreadlocks. They had enough cheek to stop and sneer at her. 'You got a hot little number there, mate,' said Dreadlocks to Merrick.

'I know that,' said Merrick pleasantly. 'I also have the make and number of that souped-up rustbucket you drive, and I have given it to the cops. They were *most* interested to hear what you'd been doing to my girlfriend here. Think about it.'

The two boys exchanged glances, made another half-hearted whistle in Peri's direction and swaggered out.

'D-do you really know their car?' asked Peri, blushing as she returned to her seat.

'No,' said Merrick, 'but I know their type. And they think I have the number, so I doubt they'll give you any more flack. In fact, I wouldn't be surprised if they left town tonight.'

Peri shook her head in bewilderment. They'd been messing up her life for weeks and Merrick had removed them, just like that!

CHAPTER

21

Peri had made her own dress to wear on the Friday night, and, expecting to be collected on Merrick's motorbike as he had suggested, made it in the form of figure-hugging culottes. A floating skirt would have been a nuisance, and besides — it wasn't Peri's style.

'A good model *looks* at home in anything,' Tory said, 'but most people find they have a particular style that seems to suit them best.' Peri wondered what hers was, and why her stepmother always pulled a wry face whenever she wore something that made her feel half-way beautiful.

After her careful preparation, it was something of a letdown when Merrick arrived quite tamely in his mother's car. 'Couldn't get my leathers over the tux after all,' he explained, 'so Ma's hitching a lift with Birdy's mum.'

Peri had been out with him for an early lunch with Parker and Tory, just before the final run-through at the CWA rooms. It had been rather a staid sort of date, but although the elder pair had seemed amused at first, they had shrugged and accepted Peri as Merrick's girl.

'Don't mind us if you feel like a cuddle on the couch,' Tory had said with a grin.

'Which means you two feel like a cuddle in the kitchen,' remarked Merrick. He did put his arm around Peri, but it was disappointingly casual and they had to rush to make the rehearsal on time.

'This party after the show,' said Merrick. 'It is okay with your parents if you go with me, Periwinkle?'

'Sure,' said Peri lightly, thinking it had better be.

After that, she had two hours to tart up for the performance and the party afterwards.

'Goodness, Peri, you look about twenty-five!' Mrs Christian sounded amused, but Peri's mirror assured her all was well. Which made it all the more galling that Merrick, although he whistled appreciatively, almost immediately turned to Mrs Christian. 'This party afterwards at Southeys',' he said, 'it might only last a couple of hours, but it could just as easily be a pretty late night.'

And if you say I can't go I'll never forgive you, thought Peri, but Mrs Christian smiled and said all right, you were only young once and perhaps he'd be good enough to keep an eye on Nicola as well. Merrick looked a bit taken aback at this and Peri glowered, but it was time they were gone, so she didn't stop to argue.

'See you soon, Skates,' she said as she went out the door.

'Weird, Periwinkle!' said Merrick. 'You say goodbye to the dog but not to your mum.'

'Stepmother.' But Peri turned and called a goodbye back over her shoulder to Mrs Christian.

Backstage Nicola was cold and shaking with stage-fright, and once more Peri, swathed in a smock to help with the make-up, found herself struck by envy. It could have been her.

God, you're so *pathetic*, thought Peri, slapping on greasepaint so viciously that Nicola squeaked with surprise.

'You'll be fine,' she told Nicola firmly. 'Just be careful you don't upstage old Paula — ' She reached out and pulled the band off Nicola's braid, tugging the strands apart and fluffing the whole mass of hair around her head. 'There — now you look practically human!' she said. 'Good luck, Nick — if you don't make a good job of it I'll — I'll —' She couldn't think of a threat dire enough, so she gave Nicola a little wave, and dropped her smock into a hamper. 'Knock 'em dead, you lot,' she said to the assembled cast, and went down the stairs to the body of the hall.

Peri and Merrick had seats in row D, which was reserved for producers, directors, sponsors, judges and their escorts. Rows A to C were empty, and so was row E, so there was no-one to distract them from what was happening on stage.

Merrick, strangely and remotely adult in a tuxedo instead of his usual jeans and sweatshirt, must have been nearly as nervous as Nicola had been, for he kept moving uneasily, crossing and recrossing his legs and tugging at his earring. In the end Peri put her hand over his and squeezed. 'It's okay,' she said. 'They'll be right.'

And they were right, on the whole.

Thousand Ships sailed smoothly along, but Peri, sitting beside Merrick, was aware of his constant tension. By now she was word-perfect in all the parts, and winced in sympathy when Menelaus missed a cue and again when Helen's wig slipped during a love scene with Paris. And Linnet Valeria put up a charming performance as Psyche, all the more remarkably because she had had to sling a coat over her costume and take official photographs of the Mayor and other guests just before she went on-stage. Larssen was with her, scribbling away in his notebook, and plonking himself in row D just as the curtain rose.

Merrick shot Larssen a hostile glance, and Peri was aware of him shifting more nervously than ever whenever Linnet was on stage. Whether his unease was personal or professional, she didn't know, but after a while he relaxed enough to twist his hand around to hold hers.

The play flew by, with Helen, now somewhat less beautiful than she had been, reclaimed by a vengeful Menelaus who had knocked his business rival's empire to smithereens with a stock-float for Trojan Horse. Peri had always wondered why Menelaus should want Helen back — after all, she'd run off quite of her own accord! But the audience seemed satisfied, and the applause for the final curtain was genuinely hearty.

Merrick went to stand with the cast for the judges' summing up, and then there was a ten minute interval while the final marks were totted up and the placings decided.

As Merrick had suspected, the *Rap Opera* won the overall prize for best play. Peri wondered if he was very disappointed, but if he was, he didn't show it. The Reef Bay Musicales won the popular vote from the audience for *Joseph and the Technicolour Dreamcoat*.

'Why?' hissed Peri. 'They weren't as good as us, or the rappers, either!'

'They chose a popular piece,' whispered Merrick. 'Most people like familiar music.'

To nobody's surprise, Linnet won the prize for the overall best actress, with the judges offering special congratulations because she had taken on the part so late. Peri thought Linnet looked as lit-up as Cass had on the Wednesday night — she looked at Cass now and found her white and exhausted, and oddly close to tears. Poor thing. Had she expected to win best actress, or was it just the let-down now the *Rap Opera* was over?

When everyone had surged to their feet and were congratulating and commiserating with one another, Peri sought out Cass.

'What's wrong?' she asked. 'You won, didn't you? Ra, ra for Scurfside High!'

'Oh — yes,' said Cass. 'It's just that it's over, I guess.' She gave a weak laugh. 'I don't know what I'm going to do with myself now, I really don't. God, Peri — I feel like I've lost something!'

'School starts soon,' reminded Peri.

Cass groaned. 'You coming back, Peri?'

'No,' said Peri. 'Probably not. I've got better things to do.'

Peri was glad about the party. It would have seemed unbearably flat to have gone straight home after the awards had been presented. The cast, declaring themselves thoroughly sick of their costumes, changed into party gear before descending on the Southey household. Peri was very satisfied with her own appearance until she saw Linnet Valeria, dressed in a swirling taffeta creation of her favourite bottle green and talking animatedly to Karl Larssen — she expected Merrick to ignore them, but he tossed Linnet several barbed remarks which she answered with familiar insults.

Uncomfortably, Peri helped herself to a glass of

sparkling wine and some food, and stood impatiently at Merrick's elbow, alternately sipping and nibbling. If he had ignored her, she thought she might have been miserable enough to seek Nicola's company, but he flicked her the occasional grin and mouthed 'Okay?' whenever he caught her eye, drawing her now and then into the conversation.

Parker Southey cruised by with a large tray of sausage rolls. 'Would you like some juice, Peri?'

'I've got a drink, thank you.'

Parker gave her a mild look through his glasses and she wondered if he was expecting her to get drunk and disorderly. Well, he could relax — tonight she was watching her step. Duncan and Debbie had returned for the big night, and she just knew Duncan was keeping his eye on her in the hopes she'd step out of line. She drained the last of her drink, collected a refill and a bunch of grapes and still had her hands full when someone put on some music. Chairs were dragged back and several couples started dancing, and Peri almost choked on her mouthful as Merrick took her arm. 'Dance, Periwinkle?'

She swallowed. 'Okay.'

He parked her glass on a table then pulled her into the gyrating crowd. They had been dancing only a few minutes when Nicola tapped Peri on the shoulder and indicated the hovering Duncan and Debbie. 'Dunc says do you want to come home with us?'

Peri shook her head emphatically but, to her

disgust, her stepbrother pushed his way over in Nicola's wake. 'I can take Peri home if you like, Merrick — I've got Nicky to drop off anyway and Debbie and I are spending the night there.'

To Peri's enormous relief Merrick drew himself up in mock indignation and said he was quite capable of getting his own date home in one piece: it was a matter of honour. Duncan looked doubtful, but Debbie tugged at his arm and eventually they took themselves off, with Nicola looking back wistfully as if she would have liked to have stayed on, too.

Another hour went by. The people who had been muttering about early mornings began to leave and the remainder broke up into the usual party factions: the earnest conversationalists, indefatigable dancers and a few more raucous types who had drunk too much and were now doing imitations in the corner. Wine and fruit juice circulated, the backstage crew thrashed out the state of the nation, more savouries appeared on the tables.

Peri danced again with Merrick, then with Menelaus, who seemed to have forgotten to go home. Someone turned the lights down and changed the music to liquid smooch. Menelaus promptly steered Peri towards Merrick, who was propped against the couch discussing ornithology with Paris. Peri slid down beside him and he put his arm round her. 'Okay, Periwinkle?' He smelt of wine and aftershave, and his earring twinkled in the glow of the lamp.

'Fine,' she said, although the smoke in the room was beginning to make her eyes sting. She had the sudden urge to touch the earring with her finger and make it swing, and wondered if perhaps she were a little drunk. It was a slow old party, but somehow just what they all needed to bring them gently back to earth. A pity though — she'd have liked to have been floating on cloud nine. She looked up at Merrick, wondering what would happen next.

Perhaps her steady regard made him uneasy, for Merrick removed his arm and took her hand instead. 'Got another dance in you, Cinderella?'

'I reckon,' she didn't want to sound too eager, but her heart thumped heavily as Merrick pulled her up and linked his arms around her waist.

'Thanks,' he whispered in her ear.

'Why?'

'For rescuing me from Paris,' he said with a snort of laughter. 'I don't know the first thing about birds.'

'Neither do I,' breathed Peri, moving closer. Over his shoulder she could see Linnet dancing with one of the sceneshifters — Larssen was watching her moodily. And then they were turning and she could no longer see Linnet.

The music ended and when Peri blinked around she saw that the room was much emptier than it had been before. Tory was half-asleep in an armchair and Parker was clearing up the dregs of the sandwiches. Paris and his wife were saying their goodbyes, and presently Linnet and Larssen announced that they were off as well. 'See you Merrick — Peri,' said Linnet casually.

'Not if I see you first, Birdy — and remind me never to direct you in anything again!'

'And *who* won best actress? C'mon Karl, time we left. And I'm driving.' The door closed behind them and Peri let out a long sigh of relief from a tension she had hardly recognised until then. The music began again, soupy and smooth, and not Peri's style at all, but just then she could have swayed to it dreamily all night. She felt Merrick's cheek on top of her head and raised her face invitingly. He kissed her and she tucked her head back against his shoulder for a long interval, but at last he stepped away and gave her a little shake. 'Wake up, Periwinkle! It's time I got you home.'

'I'm not tired.'

'I am.' And she could see the shadows under his dark eyes. Whatever reserves had kept him alert all evening seemed drained away. Parker Southey was rubbing his eyes behind his glasses and the last few diehards seemed to be leaving. Reluctantly, Peri said goodnight and followed Merrick out into the street.

The cool of the evening after the warm fug inside made her suddenly tired and shivery, but Merrick draped her coat round her shoulders. He continued to stand there, looking down at her, and Peri looked steadily back. Merrick bent his head and kissed her gently, and then much harder. She put up her hands, touched his hair, and then gently swung the earring.

'I've been wanting to do that all night,' she said.

'I suppose one seems a bit slack after the armoury you wear.'

'No — no, I like it,' she said eagerly. 'If you wear too many they get caught up in the pillow.' She blushed in the dark, hearing the crash of breakers out on the beach. 'I don't want to go home,' she said.

Merrick was still looking down at her. 'What *do* you want to do?' he asked.

'We could go back to your place?'

'I'm staying with my parents.'

'Oh.' She supposed it was the logical thing for him to be doing.

'Besides,' he said gently, 'I don't think that would be a very good idea, do you?'

He was probably right. And she wasn't drunk at all, but the combination of the night and his closeness and the euphoria of the party had made her feel relaxed and irresponsible, and she couldn't bear the idea of going home, scrubbing off her make-up and climbing into bed.

'Where is Linnet staying?' she asked.

'*Not* with my parents,' said Merrick. 'She moved out a few weeks ago. I think she's at the caravan park.'

With Karl Larssen? Peri didn't ask. 'I know what I'd like!' she said. 'I'd like to walk along the beach.'

Merrick considered the thought, tossing the car keys from hand to hand. 'Why not?' he said. 'But not here. Park and Tory might start wondering if we don't move the car.'

They drove back to Longbeach, and through the quiet streets. A cool breeze had blown up, and the beach was deserted. They got out of the car and Merrick bent to take off his shoes. 'Thank God that's over,' he said.

'The party?'

'*Thousand Ships*. Cruddy, antiquated, self-indulgent bit of trash.'

'If you hated it so much, why did you take so much trouble over it?' asked Peri.

Merrick looked down at her seriously. 'It was a job, Periwinkle. I'd rather take a cruddy theatre job in my holidays — even directing a bunch of Longbeach amateurs — than wait at tables in Sydney. But never mind that now — it's over — until the next time.'

'What will you do now?'

'After the holidays? Go back to Sydney and get on with my studies.'

'Don't you get bored? I mean — don't you feel too old to be still at school?' she said curiously.

'Sometimes,' said Merrick.

'All you get is a bit of paper at the end.'

'True. But if you're really serious about a career you owe it to yourself to grab every advantage that's going. I know I'd hate to miss out on a plum job just because I didn't have that bit of paper.'

'Oh.'

'You don't sound very convinced,' said Merrick, amused.

'I'm not. It all seems so bloody — oh, I don't know — so *useless*. Such a waste of time when you might be *doing* things.'

'Believe me, I do plenty!' objected Merrick. 'And studying's not so bad if you look at it as an interest in itself as well as a means to an end. Means to some ends, I should say, because that's what it does — it opens out your options. When you get your piece of paper you can hope for a choice instead of a single position and that's got to be to your advantage.'

'What will you do when you get your piece of paper?'

'That's easy. I'll do what seems best. It's not a bad life.' He took her hand. 'And right now it feels like a bloody good life — even if we can't top off the evening in the best way of all — in bed.'

'Why can't we?'

'Lots of reasons, Periwinkle.'

'To do with me?'

'Mostly to do with me. Let's walk.'

Swinging hands, they walked along the cold, loose sand. The wind blew in off the sea and whipped Peri's culotte dress around her legs. After a while, Merrick sat down in the shelter of a rock and she sat beside him. He kissed her, and pulled her against his side, then they sat and looked out to sea for a while before Merrick decided, firmly, that it really was time to go home.

The drive back seemed much too short, and Peri clenched her hands as the car drew up outside the silent house.

'Got your key?' he asked.

'It won't be locked.'

'No. Well ...' Merrick leaned over and released her seatbelt, then got out and opened the door for her. 'I promised Dunnycan I'd see you safely in.'

Peri shook her head. She didn't want to think about Duncan and she didn't want Merrick thinking about him either. 'I can see myself in.'

'What if those creeps are waiting about?'

'I'll spit in their bloody eyes.'

'Good girl — though I don't reckon you'll see them again. Just to be sure, I'll mention them to the cops. We can give a good description of at least two of them.' Merrick escorted her very correctly to the door, then hesitated. 'Thanks for coming, Periwinkle. I expect it was a pretty slack party by your standards?'

'No,' she said truthfully, 'I liked it.' But she'd really loved the walk on the beach and that stuff he'd said about studying opening out your options. Sure, she'd heard it all before, but Merrick wasn't just telling *her* to do it, he was doing it himself, and that made all the difference. He was such an impatient sort of person generally — he must believe in what he said or he'd never have stuck studying so long.

'Thanks,' said Merrick. 'You got me out of a hole.'

Peri pulled her coat round her and looked up at him, chilled. For the first time in almost a week she remembered why he had asked her to be his official escort that evening.

'Whose hole?' she asked abruptly. 'The one Cadence left or — or Linnet?'

Merrick stared back at her. 'You don't pull any punches, do you?'

'No.'

Merrick bent down and kissed her on the cheek. 'See you Periwinkle — and I mean that!' He turned away, but Peri had let herself into the house before he started the car.

Mrs Christian had left the kitchen light burning, but Peri went in to see Skates. He was asleep, but he sat up and yawned as Peri entered. She knelt down and hugged him, and let a couple of tears slide down her face. Just what she was crying about she wasn't sure, so she gave a gigantic sniff.

'Goodnight, Skates,' she said, but he followed her into the bathroom and watched devotedly as she peeled herself out of her culottes, put on her dressing gown, and then sat down to remove her make-up.

Her eyes looked back at her, dark, smudged and wary. Merrick hadn't answered her question, nor had he said anything concrete about seeing her again.

The whole ice-cream castle seemed to be collapsing around her ears. 'Serves me right for going off to parties with Merrick instead of taking you for a walk, huh?' she said to Skates. 'You'd never do that to *me*. Unless there was food about — you'd run off then all right and never mind poor old Peri.'

That made her laugh, and she shut Skates back in the kitchen and went to the room she shared with Nicola, who rustled up on one elbow. 'Peri —'

'What?' she said.

'Did you —'

'Yeah, yeah,' she said. 'I laid it on for half the audience and *all* the directors.'

There was a muffled giggle. 'I didn't mean that, dork! Did you like the play?'

Peri had forgotten *Thousand Ships*, but now she dredged it up. 'Yeah, it wasn't bad. You didn't fall over or anything. And you came second, overall. Nice one, Nickers.'

'Mmm.' Nicola yawned. 'Linnet was excellent, wasn't she?'

'Huh.'

'I still wish Cadi could have been in it though. She's going to feel awful when she hears how well we did. And the Surfside team.'

'Yeah — s'pose so,' said Peri shortly. She could quite see that Cadence would feel terrible about missing out on her two plum parts, but just now she was feeling pretty confused herself.

CHAPTER 22

Merrick was waiting for Peri when she came out of Tory's on Wednesday. Her spirits shot up like a rollercoaster, but she kept her face blank. 'Hi,' she said, turning briskly down the street toward the bus stop.

'Not so fast, Periwinkle,' he said with a grin. 'I've got plans for you — unless you've got to rush home?'

Peri thought about the design assignment she had to do. She had been looking forward to making a start, but there was always tomorrow. 'I'll just put these papers in my bag,' she said, 'and then I'm all yours.' She bent to put her folders in her satchel, keeping her face averted as she said, 'By the way — Linnet's working with Tory now.'

'Poor bloody Tory!' Merrick took her arm. 'I've brought the spare helmet along — fancy a spin out to the point?'

Peri put on the helmet quickly, wanting to be gone before Linnet came out. It was difficult enough working with Linnet, difficult enough seeing all the others falling over themselves to be noticed. She felt the tug of Linnet's personality, too — Linnet was fast-talking, so strong and bright — always so sure she knew where she was going. Just like Cadence, but now she'd finally broken with Merrick, Linnet didn't get under Peri's skin the way Cadence had. The way Cadence still did, if she was honest. She had gone with Nicola to the hospital again and Cadence, obviously feeling better, had talked a lot about taking stock of her life, and learning her lesson about overcommitment and honesty.

'I'll stick to my work, this year,' said Cadence, looking valiant, 'even if I have to study at home for the first few weeks.'

Yeah, yeah, thought Peri. Give Cadence Merrick five minutes back at Surfside High and she'd be prefecting, debating, librarying and all; volunteering and bulldozing just as before. Nothing could keep Cadence down for long — but you had to hand it to her, the girl had guts.

Linnet Valeria was every bit as officious, every bit as certain she was right, but somehow she was easier to take than Cadence. Maybe because she didn't look like a Barbie doll. Maybe because she was wrapped round the hunky Larssen. All the same, Peri had a gut feeling that the less Merrick saw of Linnet the better. They might have broken up, but they'd shared a lot, and all the memories must be there between them, stretched like an invisible rope.

She wondered if there were any memories left between her father and her real mother. It didn't seem likely. The first Mrs Christian had snipped the rope when she'd walked out and the bridge had tumbled into the chasm of desertion. It struck Peri suddenly that she might have other half-brothers and sisters, like Nicola, but related on the other side. She shook off that thought. One bug-eyed alien was enough.

'I'm ready,' she said, and slid onto the seat behind Merrick. She loved the motorbike, loved the power and speed and noise of it, loved the excuse to sit close and cling round Merrick's waist. 'You're still here then,' she yelled, into the wind.

'Yeah — found another directing job — a straight play over in Coral Bay.'

So he'd be able to live with his parents and commute for a few more weeks. Peri felt a lift of her spirits at the thought. Wasn't it possible he'd taken on the job at least partly to stay near her? Cautiously, the ice-cream castle began to rebuild itself in her mind.

The next week raced by. Merrick wanted to take Peri out on Saturday, but she had to turn him down.

'Tory's arranged an exotic outdoor location shoot up the coast, and she doesn't want to wait any longer — her kid's due in another couple of months.'

'Can I come too?' he suggested. 'I can admire the cheesecake!'

'Beefcake too,' said Peri. 'Don't forget Tory's got men on her books ...'

Merrick said she could call him sexist if she liked, but beefcake didn't do much for him.

'Tell you what — I'll give you a lift!' he offered.

'Can't go on the bike,' she said. 'I'm taking Skates.'

'I'll borrow Ma's car then — see you in half an hour.'

'Fine,' said Peri, and went to ring Tory and tell her she and Skates didn't need a lift. It wasn't until she had already dialed the number that she remembered Linnet would be in the party, too. But she wouldn't fret over that, not now.

The shoot was for late afternoon, when Linnet said the light would be best, so Peri and Merrick went to visit Cadence in hospital first. Peri would quite willingly have stayed away, but Merrick said he had some heart even if she hadn't, and poor old Cadi needed cheering up.

Peri said disgustedly that he sounded just like Cadence himself. Merrick laughed at her and said 'Call me Pollyanna', but she thought she saw a shadow pass over his face. He thought she was heartless. That sent a qualm through her, so she agreed to go, and contented herself with muttering crossly as she followed him into the hospital.

Later, in Mrs Merrick's old car on the way up the coast, she was so silent that Merrick glanced at her once or twice and asked if she was all right.

'Sure,' she said, but she was quaking inside. She hadn't realised his approval meant so much to her. She'd always so despised girls who gave in to their boyfriends' demands for them to drink, take drugs or have sex when they didn't want to, but now she found herself more in sympathy with their point of view. Wanting so much to please someone was a novel feeling.

Merrick drank moderately and as far as she knew he wasn't into drugs, but sex was another matter. He hadn't tried anything heavy — yet. In fact, he'd turned her down quite nicely after the party. Was that because she didn't attract him? Or was it her age? Or had he some archaic scruples about having it off with his old mate's little stepsister?

She could ask him, but once the subject was right out of the box, there'd be no putting it back. Either he'd put her off as he had before or — possibly — he might take it that she expected him to perform.

Peri frowned. At least he was old enough to know what he was doing — there'd be no clammy fumblings or stupid excuses about not wanting to buy condoms. And she was quite old enough to know what she wanted. Or who she wanted. She felt her face flush at the thought, and found herself clutching Skates' black ruff as if it were a lifeline. She forced her fingers to relax and patted him in apology. 'Merrick?' she said abruptly.

'Periwinkle?'

'I've been thinking.' She came to a stop and licked her lips. 'About what you said on the beach after the party.'

'About studying?'

'That too, but really —'

'I s'pose you'll be getting down to it in a week or so,' he said quickly. 'What is it — Year Twelve?'

'Eleven,' she said.

'Picked your courses yet?'

'Not yet.'

Somehow, the talk had skittered off on the wrong subject and Peri found it easier to let Merrick assume she would be going back to school. It wasn't really a lie, because she'd been giving it some thought.

'Hey, isn't this the turnoff?' he said. 'Have a look at the map, will you Periwinkle?'

'Oh —' Peri looked at the map. 'Yeah.' The car turned off the highway and bumped down over a rutted beach road.

'Let's get to it then,' said Merrick happily. 'Cheesecake here I come.'

'Creep.' But she let him take her hand. Let him? That was a joke. She'd have let him do a damned sight more than that, and he must know it. And on the way back she *would* talk to him seriously about that. And other things. Lots of things. Because she knew he would take her seriously and listen.

CHAPTER 23

The rest of the Tory's class had already arrived in the van and there was a holiday atmosphere as Tory was installed in a deck chair and picnic paraphernalia was set up.

Linnet Valeria, pale arms bare to the elbow, hair sparkling like copper, was fiddling with her camera and discussing wind angles — whatever they were — with Tory. She looked up as Peri and Merrick approached and Peri saw her face go still. Then she pantomimed despair and clasped her brow. 'God! This is all I need. Bloody Merrick ogling the models.'

'Too, too kind, Birdy,' said Merrick. He released Peri's arm, but not before she had felt an answering tension in his muscles at the sight of Linnet.

'Peri? Great,' said Tory. 'Leave Skates with me for now and go over with Nicholas and Shudeshka. There's some swimwear in the hamper.'

Peri changed her clothes with fingers that fumbled, then ran a comb through her hair. At Tory's nod, she and the other two students sat down on one of the rugs. 'Elbows on knees — yes, the hair's great, but shift that strand away from your face,' said Tory. 'Of course it's the photographer's job to set up the composition —'

'Too right,' said Linnet.

'But her — or his — job is made immeasurably easier if you models avoid making basic mistakes like allowing shadows to fall across your noses — yes, Nicholas, I know it's a problem! You'll find you get a lot more work if you know instinctively what to do or, at least, if that's the way it appears. Deshy, move up a bit — now — who are we waiting on?'

'Linnet,' said the two models in chorus.

Linnet hefted the camera threateningly. 'Pose,' she said.

'You always say *not* to pose —' said Nicholas, who looked like a surfie but who was hoping to get into electronics. He glanced sideways at Peri. 'These old ducks never know what they want, do they Peri?'

'I *heard* that!' said Linnet sternly. 'And I'm doing some polaroids first so you can see what not to do. Merrick — you can be my runner, since you're here. Shove that umbrella over a bit. It's about to fall down.'

'And I thought I was spectating and drooling in that order,' said Merrick.

'Great. Now some help with the mutt — Peri, can you have Skates lean against you?'

The shoot lasted two hours, and the whole time Peri's spirits sank. It was nothing she could put her finger on: Linnet and Merrick behaved impeccably, neither ignoring one another nor going into huddles, but their glances intercepted too often for Peri's comfort and sometimes, apparently unconsciously, they capped one another's remarks. Once, Merrick brushed sand off Linnet's back and shoulders as casually as if she had been his sister — or his wife.

Peri tried not to watch them, but it was impossible. Tory remained comfortably in her chair while the others packed up.

'Sometimes I wonder if babies are worth the effort,' she said to Peri. 'Could you get my jacket, please? I can't bend down.'

When Peri went to give it to her, she said casually, 'Linnet and Merrick have known one another a long time, Peri — nearly as long as Park and I.'

'It shows,' said Peri curtly. She thought again about the invisible rope of connection. No — not rope, she thought painfully — elastic. Elastic that could give and stretch but might snap back at any time.

'Yes.' Tory glanced at her and added, 'Some days I could throttle Park but even then there's something there.'

Peri nodded, then pulled on her own jacket — one she'd designed herself.

'By the by,' said Tory casually, 'there's a lingerie design competition coming up that might interest you. I'll give you the details next week.'

'Thanks,' said Peri. Her throat seemed to be closing over, but there was nothing she could do. 'Tory?'

'Yes?' she said.

There was sympathy in Tory's eyes, and Peri looked away.

'I thought I might just come to weekend classes for a bit,' she said. 'In case I decide to go back and do Year Eleven after all. It might be more interesting than Year Ten and — and Merrick says you get more choice at the end. Not that he tried to talk me into it or anything. It's just — he made me think.'

'You might like to chat to Nicholas about it — he's in nearly the same boat as you — just finished Eleven and trying to make up his mind what to do next.'

Peri shook her head. 'No, I'll make up my own mind.'

'No doubt you will,' said Tory, 'but I think it always pays to have other strings to your bow.'

'Yes,' said Peri, her eyes on Merrick. 'It does, doesn't it?'

Finally, everything was packed up. Linnet was giving the two boys a lift, the girls were going with Tory.

'Ready to roll, Periwinkle?' asked Merrick.

'Yeah. Sure thing.' She turned towards the car.

Merrick dived after her, catching her round the waist and kissing her playfully. Peri felt her insides turn to liquid, but after a moment she pulled away. 'Don't, Merrick.'

'Periwinkle?' He was looking down at her, perplexed.

Peri bit her lip. 'I don't want you to.'

Merrick looked hurt. 'Like that, is it?'

'No. Yes. I don't know.'

'Come on Periwinkle, you always know. Indecisiveness is not one of your faults.' Now he sounded sarcastic. 'So, precisely what are you objecting to? I haven't been on the garlic, and you know damned well all that about cheesecake was just a joke. Young Nicholas been giving you the eye?'

Peri's throat was closing again, but she swallowed and said ungraciously, 'I know one thing, I'm not going to hang about waiting for Linnet Valeria to call the tune.'

'Huh?' Merrick looked amused, but he was flushing too. 'Sometimes you've got to — if you don't want your head snapped off for spoiling her precious shots.'

'You know what I mean.' Peri strove to keep her voice level. 'I'm not waiting about for Linnet to decide she wants you back.'

'You reckon it's all up to her?'

'No, I don't,' said Peri honestly. 'I'm not so stupid and I don't think you're anyone's puppet. I think — I think it's a game the two of you play.'

There was a short silence.

'So who's been warning you off me, Periwinkle?' he wanted to know. 'Cadi? Or my old pal Dunnycan? Or maybe it was dear old Debs — never had much time for me, old Debs.'

'Nobody's been warning me off. I wouldn't listen if they did. It's obvious though.'

'Really.'

'Oh, come on Merrick,' she said tiredly. 'When you and Linnet get together you can see the sparks fly. God, if you looked at me the way you look at her ... You'd have taken *her* to bed after the party if she'd given the nod, wouldn't you?'

'What do you want me to say, Periwinkle?' He sounded sad and tired.

'Nothing. There's nothing you can say. And for God's sake don't give me any crap about what a nice kid I am or how you're awfully fond of me, or how I'm too young to be serious and I ought to wait for a nice boy my own age.'

'I wasn't going to.' Merrick got in the car.

'I thought that was the standard line with you older men.'

Merrick laughed, not very happily. 'Give over, Periwinkle. I'm not a bloody businessman cheating on his wife!'

'No,' she said sadly. 'But I bet you'd feel just as guilty if you'd had sex with me after the party. God, you practically came right out and said as much — you said the reasons you didn't were to do with you, not me. I just didn't realise — then — they were to do with Linnet as well.'

Merrick didn't reply.

'I don't blame you,' said Peri. 'It's been great to have someone who listens, but it isn't enough. I just can't settle for being the second string to your bow.'

Merrick nodded, but he still looked unhappy. 'Periwinkle —'

'Don't say it,' said Peri.

It was a silent drive back to Longbeach, and when they pulled up in the Christian driveway, Peri got her things together and let Skates out of the car. Then she leaned over the gearstick and kissed Merrick hard.

He looked at her in surprise. 'What was that for? I thought you reckoned I was a Bluebeard? Trying to have my cake and eat it too?'

'You never promised me anything, but you gave

me a lot, so that was a thank you — I think. For lots of things. Besides — you're bloody sexy! See you around, Merrick.'

She got out of the car. Then she went into the house and cried. And after that, she began roughing out some designs for the competition Tory had told her about. And after *that*, she told her astonished family that she was going to go back to school. Not because Merrick thought it was a good idea, she assured herself. Not because Tory advised it, but because it was best for *her*.

'But — why, Peri?' asked Mrs Christian. 'Not that we're not delighted, of course — but don't you enjoy Tory's?'

'It's great!' said Peri. 'And I'm going to go on as a weekend student when I can fit it in. But Tory's will be there for me when I finish school and get my driver's licence. And I might change my mind and want to do other things as well and I don't want to be held up just because I haven't got my little p-piece of paper.'

Her voice faltered, but even if she was rejecting the relationship Merrick was able to offer it didn't mean she had to be stupid and reject everything. He'd taught her a lot, and not only about the pitfalls of romance.

'Studying opens out your options,' she said, aware she was quoting him. 'When you get your piece of paper you can hope for a choice instead of just a single position. And I want to have a choice. I want to have a second string, not just one.'

Her family was still staring, so she made herself grin. 'Besides — Cadence Merrick says Ms Borrojavic's staying on as Speech and Drama teacher at Surfside High — I reckon I might just learn something — who knows? There might be another show coming up! And I've got to keep the bug-eyed alien under control — she's getting too bloody cocky after *Thousand Ships*. And ...' She knew she was babbling, and bent to stroke Skates.

'Point made, Peri,' said Mrs Christian quietly. 'You're going back to school and it's your own decision, and you don't give a stuff whether we, or anyone else, are pleased or not. You're doing it for *you*, right?'

'Wrong. I gotta date with a lump of chewie.'

'Are you sure you can handle Tory's and school?' asked Mr Christian. 'Year Eleven's no game.'

Peri grinned at him painfully. 'You better believe it!' she said. 'Give us Christians something to work for and a bit of peace now and again and we can handle the bloody world! Right, Nickers?'

Nicola nodded nervously, her hair fluffing around her pointy little face.

'Hey — did I tell you lately your hair looks crappy?' asked Peri.

Nicola gulped. 'I guess so. You always do.'

'In this case,' said Peri grandly, 'I lied. Feel like coming for a walk with me and Skates?'

'What for?' asked Nicola.

'To talk,' said Peri. 'Just to talk.'